The Po

by

Máirín Johnston

Mary O'Neill
10 yrs Old
P7
27/10/a8
01861 551087

H. P. C

Attic Press
Dublin

First Published in 1993 by
Attic Press
4 Upper Mount Street
Dublin 2

British Library Cataloguing in Publication Data
Johnston, Mairin
Pony Express
I. Title
823.914

ISBN 1-85594-087-6

The right of Mairin Johnston to be identified as the author of this work has been asserted in accordance with the Copyright, Designs and Patents Act, 1988.

Cover Illustration: Angela Clarke
Origination: Verbatim Typesetting & Design
Printing: Guernsey Press

Dedication

For my Grandson, Cian

Acknowledgements

My very special thanks to Therese Cunningham of the Dublin Society for the Prevention of Cruelty to Animals who kindly provided me with factual information on the traffic in live horses for slaughter abroad. I am also indebted to Clodagh Corcoran and Joan Somers for their help and advice and to Roy Johnston who came to my assistance when technology let me down. My gratitude also to the staff of the National Library and the Government Information Services. Finally, I would like to thank all in Attic Press, for their unswerving support and encouragement.

Máirín Johnston,
August 1993

About the Author

Born in 1931, Máirín Johnston grew up in the heart of the Liberties, where her family on her mother's side had lived since 1850 and on her father's side since 1680. She attended St Brigid's National School, the Coombe, until she was 14 years of age. Until her marreage in 1952, she worked in various shirt factories and in Jacob's Biscuit Factory. Her main intersts are music, politics, literature, the women's movement and social history. She is the mother of two girls and two boys. In 1983 her book, *Around the Banks of Pimlico*, was published. It immediately reached the bestsellers list and remained there for more than two months. She is currently researching her next publication.

History of Pony Express

Before the outbreak of World War Two, exports of live Irish horses to the Continent for slaughter numbered only about two dozen horses a week. After the war, the demand for horseflesh in France, Belgium, Italy and Holland increased to such an extent that by 1949 the export numbers had leaped to 29,331!

There was a number of reasons for this enormous increase. Thousands of Irish horses had become redundant due to the introduction of the tractor. This little machine, with its fork-lift and auxiliary implements, could do the work of sixteen men and get the work done in half the time. Motorised vans and lorries replaced horse-drawn vehicles and the motor-car ousted the family pony and trap. As a result, horses of every description (other than the racing variety) suffered from abandonment and neglect.

In spite of constant pressure from animal welfare societies, the plight of the horses was ignored over the years by successive governments, who also refused enterprising business people permission to open abattoirs for the slaughter, freezing and canning of horsemeat for human consumption abroad. This was due to a combination of economic short-sightedness and a powerful beef lobby that saw the export of horsemeat as a threat to their profits.

The market was wide open for unscrupulous horse-buyers to exploit the situation, which they did in a most cruel and ruthless manner. Exporting horses on the hoof became a highly profitable business. The numbers being shipped abroad became a cause for concern and many people expressed the fear that the country was fast being cleaned out of horses, ponies and donkeys. In certain areas in the west of Ireland, where tractors could never be used, farmers complained that they were unable to compete with the Pony Express buyers who were paying £50 for horses usually sold for £10.

Ostensibly, the horses were going to the Continent to work. They were also supposed to be fit to travel and be not more than fifteen years of age. In practice these regulations were ignored. The conditions down on the docks were appalling. There was no provision for feeding and no shelters for the horses, who sometimes had to stand in biting winds for many hours waiting for veterinary examinations. Added to this they were scared stiff by loud noises and the cranes swinging horses onto the boats.

The inhumane conditions under which the horses were exported gave rise to widespread concern and a campaign was launched by the Dublin Society for the Prevention of Cruelty to Animals (DSPCA), the International League for the Protection of Horses (ILPH), the Dublin Animal Protection Society (DAPS) and Our Dumb Friends' League (ODFL). Many well-known personalities and a few politicians, notable Alderman Alfie Byrne TD, Maurice Dockrell TD, Michael ffrench-O'Carroll TD and Senator Sheehy-Skeffington, also worked tirelessly over the years to bring about legislative change.

In 1952, a young Canadian reporter named Patrick Keatley, a special correspondent with the *Manchester Guardian*, came to Ireland to write a series of articles for his paper on the Pony Express. These described in detail and with photographs the appalling conditions at the docks, on the boats and on the trains, and the cruelty with which the horses were slaughtered on the Continent. These articles were reprinted by *The Irish Times*.

When in 1955 the Post Office decided to replace its horses with motor transport, Nancie Hatte of the DSPCA organised a fund to buy all the horses. This she eventually did. In 1957 the government at last agreed to permit the export of horseflesh to the Continent and promised to start a new industry but in 1958 there was still no factory.

Disappointed and frustrated at the long delay, a group of concerned and enterprising women, led by Mrs MacNeill, decided in 1959 to raise the necessary sum to purchase premises to start an abattoir and asked the public to take out five-shilling shares in the project. It was called the Irish Horse Abattoir Investment Co Ltd.

At the end of December 1959 one of the worst disasters on board the Pony Express took place. Horses en route to France on board the *City of Waterford* met with severe gales and forty-seven horses were lost at sea. Another eleven had to be shot on arrival. During the month of January, the Irish and British press printed stories on two further shipments which met icy weather. The rail journey to Paris took eighteen hours and many of the horses arrived dead or dying.

Throughout 1960, the campaign against the horse traffic gathered momentum in a blaze of publicity. In November of that year, the government announced that as and from 1st December, horses would be shipped to the Continent only under licence and that a condition of the licence would be that all horses shipped must be killed within thirty miles of the port of entry. At the same time the government announced that an abattoir to kill large numbers of horses for export as meat would be started in 1961 and that when this was functioning, the export of horses of seven years and over would be prohibited.

Meanwhile, the women of the Irish Horse Abattoir Investment Co. were in business. Their factory was up and running at Turnings Lower, Straffan, Co Kildare. They showed that a group of determined women can overcome the most appalling difficulties. In Limerick another private abattoir was opened.

In spite of government promises, the horse traffic continued and in 1961 nearly 10,000 horses were shipped to France for slaughter. The ban on the shipment of horses of seven years and over didn't come into effect until November 1961.

When, in March 1963, an order came into effect that horses shipped to the continent for slaughter must be under five years, shipments to France ceased.

Finally, at the beginning of 1965, the then Minister for Agriculture, Mr Charles Haughey, made an order that as and from March 1965, no horse of any age could be shipped for slaughter to the continent.

The Pony Express had finally come to an end but it had taken twenty years of hard and consistent campaigning on the part of all the animal humane societies and their supporters throughout the country to bring this about.

A major contribution was made by Mrs MacNeill and her band of courageous women who proved that it was possible to use up surplus horses here by killing them humanely in her abattoir and exporting the horseflesh, thus saving the horses the long, harrowing journey to a foreign country.

Since January 1992, new EC regulations have been in force, allowing the free movement of horses between member states. Fears have been expressed by animal welfare societies and other organisations and individuals that because the regulations aren't strict enough there could be a recurrence of the Continental slaughter trade. The current EC Council directive will be reviewed next September.

One

The bus was late and the sky threatened rain. Kate Doyle looked anxiously up the Emmet Road, wishing the bus would appear. At the top of the hill, near Murray's Lane, a slight bend in the road limited her view. She wondered if she should walk home. It wasn't all that far and her mother had warned her not to delay too long in her Aunt Mary's. But she didn't want to get wet and if she left the bus-stop the bus would be sure to come. That was always the way, she reasoned.

The threepenny bit Aunt Mary had given her was making her hand feel hot and sticky. She was about to have a look at the tempting array of jars in the window of a nearby sweet shop when the noise of hooves and shouting caught her attention. Coming round the bend in the road was one of the strangest sights she had seen in all her thirteen years.

A troop of donkeys, tied together in pairs, followed by two ponies, came plodding down the hill towards her, heading for the city. Some of the animals looked exhausted, but even so, six rough-looking men, wielding birch rods, urged them on with switches and shouts. Kate counted twelve donkeys in all. Two of them, she noticed, had no shoes and limped painfully along.

A mixture of anger and pity brought the tears to Kate's eyes. She wanted to tell the men to stop but she was afraid. Not many people were about, but those who were just stood and stared, unwilling to get involved. Suddenly a frail old woman standing at the bus stop, stepped forward and begged the men to 'show a bit of mercy to the poor, dumb creatures'. In reply, one of them uttered a string of abusive words and told her in no uncertain terms to mind her own business.

'That's exactly what I am doing, you impudent young cur,' she shouted back, brandishing an umbrella threateningly. 'You ought to be ashamed of yourselves, so you should, walloping defenceless animals like that. What class of a rearing did you get at all?' Her face was almost purple with indignation.

'Pay no attention to them, mam,' advised a man standing beside Kate. 'They're nothing but a bunch of bowsies. Anyway, it's not worth while upsetting yourself over them poor nags because they'll soon be taken out of their misery. They're obviously on their way to Keefe's the Knackers in Newmarket.'

'Indeed and they are not,' the old woman replied sharply, 'and furthermore, I know for a fact that their misery is only beginning. Them unfortunate animals are bound for the docks to board the Pony Express along with hundreds of others and if something isn't done to stop it soon, there won't be a horse left in the country.'

'The Pony Express? Never heard of it. Is it new?'

12

The man was highly amused at the name, but the old woman seemed not to notice.

'New? It's anything but,' she replied emphatically. 'That's been going on for the last six years — in fact, ever since the war ended in 1945, and the numbers are increasing every year. Sure last year alone, twenty-two-and-a-half thousand were export- ed. What beats me is that they can get away with it.'

'Don't mind me asking you mam, but where exactly are these animals going?'

'To the Continent to be slaughtered! But they're supposed to be going to work, God bless the mark. Work is right. You can see for yourself that some of them can hardly walk, never mind work.'

'But surely, if it's as bad as you say, the government would do something about it.'

'Ah, the government my foot. Sure the best part of them fellas are big cattle farmers interested only in protecting the beef trade. They know well what's going on but because it suits their pockets, they're not going to stop it. It's a crying disgrace, so it is.'

'Is that a fact? Don't mind me asking you, but how did you find out about it?' Something in the man's tone made Kate suspect that he was only humouring the old woman. She, however, was delighted by his apparent interest.

'Isn't it in all the papers for the last couple of weeks. There's only ructions down below at the North Wall every day with pickets from different animal welfare societies protesting. Sometimes, if they have the money, they buy some of the animals before they go on board, but they can't buy them all — there's too many. And anyway, that's not the answer. The only right thing to do is to bring the Pony Express to a halt. There'll be blood spilled over it yet, mark you me.'

The bus arrived and Kate heard no more but she had heard enough to arouse her interest. She wondered if her father knew about this Pony Express. He must, because he always read the *Evening Mail*. Yet she'd never heard him mention anything about it.

As the bus passed the troop, she took another good look. She knew enough about horses to be able to tell that most of the donkeys, and certainly the two ponies, were too good for the knacker's yard.

All the way home she wondered what happened to the animals when they reached the Continent. And what did the old woman mean when she said that their misery was only beginning?

'What in the name of fortune kept you?' her mother demanded as soon as she got in the door. 'I thought I told you not to delay. Your father will be in any minute and the spuds aren't even washed. You better get them on quick.'

Kate looked over at the window where her younger brother, Jamie, sat reading an *Our Boy's* magazine. She was about to ask why *he* couldn't have washed the spuds but thought better of it. It would only start a row. Besides, other things were on her mind. As soon as she had the potatoes scrubbed she began telling her mother about the donkeys and what the old woman had said about the Pony Express.

'The Pony Express,' exclaimed Jamie, who had been only half listening. 'That's the name of a cowboy film.

14

Remember we saw it down in the Tivo. It was great.'

'Cowboy film is right,' said his mother with a laugh. 'Mind you, there are plenty of cowboys involved in this Pony Express but they're not the glamorous Hollywood variety. A load of crooks, that's what they are.'

The loud barking of a dog outside in the yard sent Kate's mother into a flurry of activity. 'Merciful heavens, there's Nipper — your father's back.'

Jamie jumped up, opened the half-door, and was immediately pounced on by his mongrel pet. A pony and float had pulled into the cobbled yard outside the cottage and as Mr Doyle jumped down and tied the reins loosely around one of the shafts, the two youngest children, Nora and Whacker, ran to greet him.

'You can close the gate, Jamie,' his father shouted above all the noise and confusion, 'and unyoke Amber immediately.' The smell of fried mackerel wafted across the yard and Mr Doyle licked his lips. 'Mmm, that's a lovely smell, Madge,' he commented to Mrs Doyle as he entered the kitchen. 'I'm famished with the hunger — which reminds me, Kate, you'd better check that there's a salt-lick hanging up for Amber. She was sweating a lot today.'

He threw himself down heavily into an armchair and immediately Nora and Whacker began to untie his boots while their mother attended to the meal. Having filled a basin with hot water for her father's feet, Kate went outside to feed Amber.

The three-year-old filly was Kate's pet. It had been bought from Buck Fowler, a neighbour, just as soon as it was ready to leave its mother. Kate's father, whose skill in such matters was locally renowned, came to help the mare at the birth. He took Kate with him and she was delighted when the tiny, wet foal staggered to its feet moments after it was born. For Kate, this wonderful experience marked the beginning of her passionate love for all horses and for the little foal in particular.

She christened it Amber, because of its beautiful, dark-chestnut coat. Every evening, when her father returned from his deliveries around the city, Kate watered and fed the filly and gave her a good brush down. On weekends she gave a much more thorough grooming, especially if the family was taking a trip out the country in the trap. On these occasions, Kate plaited Amber's long, black mane, winding each plait into a tight knob at the root of the hair. Her tail was set into shape with the aid of a tail bandage and her hooves were scraped and oiled. Even when pulling the float, Amber was much admired, but when she was between the shafts of the trap, people stopped and stared.

This evening Kate got through her tasks quickly because she was anxious to ask her father about the Pony Express. She knew that he liked to have his dinner in peace so she waited for an opportune moment to broach the subject.

'Yes, right enough, I've been reading all about it in the evening papers and very grim reading it is, too. Some of the poor animals die during the crossing and have to be thrown overboard, others die on arrival and some have to be killed at the quayside. You see, horses suffer terrible from sea-sickness, and the conditions on board the Pony Express are appalling.'

'For goodness sake, Danny,' gasped Mrs Doyle in horror, 'will you have a bit of cop-on. You'll frighten the life out of Kate with that kind of talk. Can't you see you're upsetting her?'

Kate was indeed upset but she wanted to hear more. 'Who is sending the animals away, da, and why?'

'Well, Kate,' said her father, reaching up to take his pipe off the mantelpiece, 'the boss of the Pony Express is a man called Mr Big. It's not his real name but he's called that because he talks big, acts big, and has a big bank balance. He's also a big horse-breeder and lives in a big country estate outside the city.

At this point, Mr Doyle bent over, stuck a twisted piece of paper into the fire and began to light his pipe. When he finally spoke, he avoided looking at Kate. 'The reason they're sent is to provide cheap protein for the people on the Continent. In other words they eat them.'

Kate eyes opened wide in disbelief. She covered her face with her hands. 'They eat horses! Yuck, that's disgusting.' She felt she was going to be sick.

'Now look what you've done, Danny,' cried Mrs Doyle. 'You ought to have more sense than to be telling the child things like that. She's too young to understand that kind of talk.'

'What's wrong with telling her the truth?' said Kate's father indignantly. 'She asked, didn't she? And she's no child any more, you know. In six months she'll be fourteen and out earning her living. You can't wrap her in cotton wool and expect her to survive out there in the jungle. Anyway, she eats cows, lambs, pigs and chickens. What's the differ between them and a horse?'

A dead silence greeted this question. It was something that Mrs Doyle had never thought of before. Kate took her hands from her face and sat down on a form by the fire, looking forlornly into the flames. Then turning to her father she asked, 'But, if what you say is true, da, why isn't something done to stop the Pony Express? I thought there was a law against cruelty to animals.'

'Easier said than done,' said Mr Doyle, pressing the tobacco down into the bowl of his pipe with the handle of his penknife.

'You see, Kate, it's a bit complicated to explain and I don't really know all the ins and outs myself. What I do know, however, is that a lot of influential people are involved — people with money, business people, and people in politics. The law turns a blind eye to them.' He spat contemptuously into the fire and sent sparks sizzling up the chimney.

Mrs Doyle sat down at the foot sewing-machine by the window and sighed. She wished that Kate would show as much interest in the sewing as she did in the horses. After a few minutes her temper got the better of her and she called out impatiently, 'Look here, Kate, if you've nothing better to do, you can give me a hand with this skirt. It's high time you learned to make a buttonhole. When it comes to looking for a job, horses aren't going to be much use to you. There's that machine there and you can't even thread it.'

'You'd better go and help your mother,' said Mr Doyle with a smile. Kate threw her eyes up to heaven. Nothing bored her more than sewing and the thought of having to work at it for a living threw her into a depression.

'I'll tell you what, Kate,' said her father sympathetically. 'I've to drop in tomorrow to see Ned Coyne, the blacksmith. He's the very man that'll tell you all about the Pony Express. Why don't you come around with me? That's if your mother doesn't need you to help with the sewing,' he added hastily, seeing the look of disapproval on Mrs Doyle's face. Kate gave him a grateful smile. At least he understood how she felt.

As far as her mother was concerned, however, feelings didn't come into it. It was simply a foregone conclusion that Kate would follow in her footsteps and take up the tailoring after leaving school. It was, after all, a good, clean, useful job, and with piece-work, not badly paying. Best of all, Kate could continue it at home after marriage, just like herself. What more could a young girl want? To Kate's mother, this wasn't a question — it was an answer.

That night Kate lay awake listening to the wind and the rain, worrying about the donkeys tossing about on the Irish sea. If only the wind would stop. She hoped none of the horses would die and have to be thrown overboard. Her compassion for the suffering animals wouldn't allow her to accept even the throwing of the dead horses into the sea. In her imagination she saw it happen and she clasped her hands to her face to block out the scene. It was too terrible to contemplate. Then the vision of the donkeys and ponies on their way to the docks that afternoon began to torment her. How could men be so cruel, she asked herself again and again. Surely there was some way of stopping the Pony Express? It worried her that her father didn't think it possible. Maybe Ned Coyne thought differently. Tomorrow would tell.

Two

Kate woke up next morning feeling tired after a fitful sleep. It was Saturday and she was glad there was no school. Nora lay beside her in the bed, fast asleep. Against the opposite wall was another bed where Jamie and Whacker slept. She could hear her mother moving about in the kitchen preparing the breakfast, and the noise of her father's hobnailed boots outside on the cobbled yard. It was time to get up. Careful not to wake Nora, she eased herself out of the bed and dressed quickly before going over to rouse Jamie. The room was tiny, with enough space only for the two single iron beds and a chest of drawers. The ends of the beds were covered with the children's clothes and under each bed was a bucket.

On the other side of the kitchen was her parents' bedroom. The lavatory was inconveniently situated outside in the yard and was shared by Kate's grandparents, who lived in the cottage next door. The Doyles had lived here for generations and although they moaned about the lack of space and other facilities, they wouldn't dream of moving out. From here, Kate's father carried on the traditional family business. A painted sign on the two big wooden gates into the yard read: Danny Doyle & Son, Haulier, Nos. 7-8, Summer Street South, Dublin.

After breakfast, Kate fed Amber and harnessed her for the float. Saturday was a very busy day for her father. He had to be over in the vegetable market early to get the best of the produce for his customers. Jamie always went with him — reluctantly, unlike Nipper, who trotted along happily under the float, his tongue wagging at one end of his body and his bushy tail at the other. As soon as they had departed, Kate began mucking out the stable and laying down clean straw. While she was hosing down the yard, she saw her mother go into her grandparents' cottage to light the fire and cook their breakfast. She did this every morning. It was her way of thanking them for helping her with the children.

Nora and Whacker were only getting up when Kate finished her work outside. Her mother had already begun the Saturday morning ritual of cleaning the cottage inside and out, and the smell of carbolic soap and Jeyes' Fluid hung heavy on the air.

'I want you to run down to Bridie Fay's for a few ham-parin's and sausages, Kate. Make sure they're lean. Your granny wants a half-ounce of brown snuff in Reilly's and granda wants an ounce of Ruddel's twist tobacco. Don't delay talking to any of your pals because I want to get the coddle on by eleven.'

Kate was only too glad to be released from the housework. She loved the Saturday morning atmosphere in Meath Street with everything all hustle and bustle. By the time she reached Reilly's the tobacconist, she was in a relaxed, happy mood. The shop was empty and she had to ring the little bell on the counter to announce her presence. While she waited, her eyes roamed casually over the morning newspapers on display. Suddenly her eye caught a report under the heading: 'A 700-mile Journey to Slaughter.'

Kate began to read.

Paris, 23 June 1952. At 10.43 on a sunny morning here a few days ago, the crumpled form of a little black mare twitched in the swelling pool of her own blood on an abattoir floor. Then abruptly, there was a shudder and she lay still. For Minstrel Girl it was the end of the trail, an agonising trail that had begun in County Galway five days ago. Or was it quite the end? They said that the captive-bolt killer was almost instant-aneous, but her eyes were still bright and wide open as a lanky French butcher . . .

Kate couldn't go on. Her eyes were blurred with tears.

Miss Reilly appeared from the back room. 'Hello Kate. You're a sight for sore eyes. Only for your red hair and freckles I wouldn't know a bit of you. Honest to God, but you're getting as big as a house. And what can I do for you, dear?'

She spoke in a refined accent which always amused Kate. Today, however, Kate was too upset to notice. When she opened her own mouth to ask for the snuff and tobacco, she sounded as though she was talking through her nose. Miss Reilly looked at her enquiringly.

'Are you all right, my dear? You seem to be nursing a very bad cold. Here, suck one of these lozengers. It'll help to clear the tubes.'

While Miss Reilly was weighing the snuff, Kate made a decision. 'Could I have this newspaper as well, Miss Reilly? I think I have enough money for everything.'

'Well, my dear, even if you haven't, your mother's custom is good. Nice to see you and give your mother my regards.'

Kate thought she'd never get out of the shop. She raced all the way home and looked so flushed that her mother told her to sit down.

'I know I told you to hurry but I didn't mean you to kill yourself. It's either a feast or a famine with you. What's that you have there? The morning paper! What in the name of fortune possessed you to buy that?'

Kate explained about the article, adding, 'I'll pay you back for the paper when da gives me my pocket money today. I just had to buy it.'

She spread the paper out on the kitchen table and began to read the article aloud. It described in lurid terms every detail of Minstrel Girl's final moments. The reporter had traced the five last days of the little black mare and 106 of her companions, from the west of Ireland to the French slaughterhouse. They had boarded a Dutch motorship at Drogheda on Friday and didn't reach the abattoir in Paris until the following Tuesday. During the ninety-six-hour journey none of the horses slept and on the train journey from Dieppe to Paris they had no food or water.

There was a long silence when Kate finished reading. All her mother could do was shake her head from side to side. When she looked at Kate's face she was moved by her expression of deep sadness.

'Listen Kate,' she said gently, 'you're only beginning to learn just how cruel life is. You mustn't let it get in on you, or you'll make yourself sick. I know it's hard, but you're going to have to forget all this because there's nothing you or I can do about it.'

'But how can I forget about it, ma? The reporter said that last year 10,397 horses had gone to France and another 9,000 to Belgium. Just imagine, all those horses. The old woman was right. At this rate there won't be a horse left in the country. It says here that this is the first of a series of articles to let people know what's going on. We'll have to make sure to buy the paper every week.'

The sound of the pony and cart coming into the yard put an end to the conversation.

'Here's your father now and the table isn't even laid. Hurry up and pour that kettle of hot water into the basin. Put a drop of cold in so that it's not too hot — he was nearly scalded yesterday.'

Kate ignored her mother's fussing. She knew her father never noticed whether the table was laid or not. While her mother served the coddle with an enormous enamel ladle, her father and Jamie entertained them all with funny stories about the market and the people they met. Kate wished the meal was over so that she could show her father the paper.

As was the custom every Saturday after dinner, the children gathered around their father with faces wreathed in smiles. It was pocket-money time. Each one received an amount according to age, with extras for special jobs done during the week. They raced out immediately to buy their favourite sweets and comics. When they had gone, Kate produced the newspaper. Mr Doyle's face looked very grave after he had finished reading the report. 'You did right to buy the paper, Kate. Things are an awful lot worse than I ever imagined.'

He stood up and reached for his jacket. 'Come on. Get Amber out of the stable. It's time we got ourselves around to the forge. Ned Coyne's the man to wise us up on all this. He hears about everything that stirs in the horse-trade.'

Kate rode Amber around to the forge, her father leading the filly by a rope attached to the head-collar. She could hear the ringing sound of the hammer on the anvil long before they arrived. There was no one in the forge but Ned and his son. In spite of the blazing fire, it seemed dark inside at first but gradually her eyes became accustomed to the gloom. It amused Kate the way the two men greeted each other like long-lost friends although they saw each other frequently. When she slid down off the filly, Ned stood back in mock-surprise and took stock of her.

'Well, by jingo, if it isn't Kate. She's the spit of you, Danny — only better looking. And I can see she's a horsewoman in the making, able to ride barebacked, no less.' Kate blushed at the compliments and the two men laughed.

'Looks as though you're having a slack time today, Ned. You're usually busier on Saturdays.'

'Ah, with the way things are going, I'm lucky to be earning anything at all, Danny. It's what they call progress. All this new-fangled machinery on the farms and the like. The horse is becoming redundant and it's affecting everyone in the trade. Everyone that is, except Mr Big, the boss of the Pony Express.'

'Now isn't that a coincidence,' exclaimed Kate's father. 'That's the very thing I want to talk to you

about. Did you see that bit in the newspaper this
morning? Read it out there, Kate, and tell Ned what
you saw yesterday coming down the Emmet Road.'

Ned and Mr Doyle sat puffing their pipes while
Kate read and told her story. When she finished, Ned
stood up and patted her on the shoulder. 'I know
you're upset, Kate, at the thought of all this cruelty,
but don't despair. Something is being done about it.
Take a look at this.'

He went over to a shelf on the wall and took down
a printed leaflet.

'You can have that — it's all about a protest parade
that's to take place through the city this day week.
I've a bundle of them here that I've to distribute to my
customers. Maybe you'd like to lend a hand? All
you'd have to do is give one to all the neighbours
who have horses and ask for their support.'

Kate was overjoyed. At last she was able to do
something. She felt very important as she took the
leaflets from Ned Coyne.

'Is it all right if I go around with them now, da,
while Amber is being shod?'

'Off with you and don't be long, but before you go
you'd better give me one for myself. And,' he added
with a chuckle, 'you'd better go straight back home
when you've finished or you'll land the two of us in
the dog-house.'

Kate was nearly quarter-ways through the leaflets
when she met one of her friends, Lila Keogh. When
Lila heard what she was doing, she offered to lend a
hand and between the two of them the job was done
in no time. Much to Kate's surprise, she discovered
that a number of the horse-owners had no interest
whatsoever in the Pony Express and that others even

approved of it!

Her father had arrived home just before her so she went into Amber's stable to have a look at the filly's new shoes. While she was there she heard the crack of a whip and the familiar voice of Buck Fowler roaring at Dusty. Thrusting her head out over the half-door she saw Buck trying to manoeuvre a small cart full of scrap into the yard. Kate drew back quickly so that Buck wouldn't see her. His was the only yard she hadn't gone to with a leaflet. It wouldn't have been any use. Buck didn't like animals and showed it by his cruelty to Dusty. Kate watched him descend with difficulty from the shaft of the cart. On his left foot he wore a big, black surgical boot. He limped and staggered over towards the cottage door.

'Drunk again,' Kate muttered in disgust. She decided to wait until Buck had gone but he seemed to be in no hurry. Distributing the leaflets had filled her with a great sense of achievement and she wanted to tell her father what the people had said. She was also hoping that there might be other things she she could do to make herself useful for the protest campaign.

'Why did Buck have to come just now?' she sighed impatiently. 'He's nothing but a blinking nuisance.'

Although she wasn't aware of it until later, Buck's unwelcome arrival with Dusty was to provide her with all the reasons necessary for becoming more personally and more deeply involved in the protest against the Pony Express.

Three

Buck had called to ask Kate's father for the loan of the float on Monday night. He needed it to move the furniture of a local family to a Corporation house in Crumlin. It was a chance for him to earn five shillings and he didn't want to miss it. Always willing to help Buck, Mr Doyle agreed readily.

Outside in the stable, Kate was torn between wanting to remain out of sight until Buck's departure and wanting to say hello to Dusty. The little mare stood in the yard, her head hanging down, looking thoroughly miserable. Kate couldn't bear it any longer. She emerged from the stable with Amber in tow. At the sight of her filly foal, Dusty lifted her head and whinnied softly, before giving Amber an affectionate face-lick.

Kate was appalled at Dusty's neglected appearance. Her coat was dull and caked with mud and her tail and mane were a mass of tangles. Buck's callous indifference towards her made Kate's blood boil. She felt that he had no right to have Dusty if he wasn't willing to look after her properly. In the past, her father's reprimands had brought only temporary improvement but he had been so busy lately he hadn't been able to keep an eye on Dusty. Something would have to be done about Buck's cruelty, she resolved, but what she did not know.

She was filling a bucket with water for Dusty when Jamie came racing into the yard with Nipper at his heels. He stopped dead when he saw the cart full of scrap.

'Boy, oh, boy. Look at that.' Jamie rubbed his palms together and his eyes lit up with delight. 'I wonder if there are any pram-wheels or axles in there for my box-car.' He looked around conspiratorially and whispered, 'Ay Kate, where's Buck?'

'He's in the house, and don't you go poking about among his scrap or he'll beat the living daylights out of you — and so will da.'

Jamie ignored the advice and began rummaging through the scrap, until his experienced eye caught sight of two small gig-wheels, which he swooped upon with joy. In a flash he had them hidden under a bale of straw. He was about to resume his searching when his attention was drawn to Nipper, who was sniffing and whining around Dusty's front feet. Jamie got down on his hunkers to investigate but drew back quickly, holding his nose.

'Janey Mac! Kate, come here and have a decko at this. There's something wrong with Dusty's hooves. The stink would knock you down.'

Kate was quick to realise that something was seriously wrong.

'Get da quick,' she cried, but at that very moment the door opened and her father emerged. She called and beckoned to him to come quickly. Buck limped slowly behind, dragging his big boot with difficulty as he tried hard to maintain his balance.

Running her hand down the back of Dusty's leg, Kate grasped the fetlock firmly and made a clicking sound with her tongue. The mare obediently raised her foot. Her father peered closely at the hoof and told Kate to lift up the other one. Then he stood up and turned angrily on Buck. 'How long has she been like this?' he demanded. Buck shrugged his shoulders.

'I haven't a clue — there was nothing wrong with her this morning. She must've just picked up something somewhere.' He averted his eyes from Mr Doyle's steady gaze and shifted uneasily on his feet.

'Get her home quick,' Mr Doyle ordered. 'That unfortunate animal has a very bad dose of thrush and she didn't get it today nor yesterday. She needs treatment straight away. Straight away now. Do you hear?' He thrust his face close to Buck's, shouting the last words. Buck didn't seem in the least bit intimidated by this outburst.

'Thrush!' he repeated scornfully. 'Aw, come on now Danny, who are you trying to kid? Sure that's nothing. By the way you're talking, you'd think she had foot-and-mouth disease.'

'Don't try to act the innocent with me, Buck,' replied Kate's father. 'You know very well how serious this is. Her feet could be permanently damaged. I've warned you before about neglecting Dusty but this time you're going a bit too far. Now, get the vet, or else I won't be responsible for my actions.'

For a moment Buck was stunned into silence by Mr Doyle's threatening tone. He was also embarrassed at being told off in front of Kate and Jamie, and fancied they were grinning at his discomfort.

'Ah, for God's sake, Danny, have a heart. Can't you see for yourself that the oul nag has had her day? What's wrong with her is old age. In fact, last week I happened to mention to a guy in the scrapyard that I was strongly thinking of selling her to Keefe's the Knackers but he said that I'd get more for her from the Pony Express. The Pony Express, for God's sake! Did you ever hear the like in all your life?' He threw back his head with a loud laugh, displaying a mouthful of black teeth.

Kate could hardly believe her ears. Sell Dusty to the Pony Express! Buck must be out of his mind.

'You can't do that, Buck,' she burst out. 'Dusty is a lovely pony. She only looks old because you don't treat her properly. All she needs is someone to take care of her.' She put her arms around Dusty's neck and looked besceechingly at her father. 'Tell him, da. Tell him about the Pony Express.'

Mr Doyle patted the mare on the flank. 'Kate is right,' he said. 'Dusty can't be allowed to go to the knackers' yard or the Pony Express either; she's a good young working mare, with plenty of years still ahead of her.'

Kate looked defiantly at Buck. 'See, you think you can do what you like, but you can't. My da will ...'

Before she could say another word, her father interrupted. 'That's enough, Kate. Yourself and Jamie had better go inside. I'll sort this out with Buck.'

Although her father agreed with Kate, he wouldn't allow her to speak in such a fashion to any grown-up, no matter how much in the wrong they might be.

Kate knew she was being put in her place. Her

cheeks burned as she saw the look of triumph in Buck's leering expression. Out of earshot she muttered to Jamie, 'In other words, children should be seen and not heard.'

Mr Doyle turned to Buck. 'Now listen here Buck, you can't be serious about selling Dusty. It's the daftest thing I ever heard you say. How do you think you'll earn a living without her? Honest to God, but I'm beginning to think that you need your head examined.'

Buck took advantage of Mr Doyle's more conciliatory tone. 'Well, it's just like this, Danny, if it's a question of spending money on her, or getting money for her, I've no choice. I can't afford a vet — it's as simple as that, see.'

'Right. I understand about the cost of the vet but you could've avoided the thrush in the first place by taking better care of the pony. You know as well as I do that grooming is essential and that her hooves need picking out every day. It's obvious by the look of her that you do neither one nor the other and, as for the condition of her coat, I really don't know what to say.'

Before Buck could reply, Mrs Doyle poked her head over the half-door to announce that tea was ready. A look of relief came over Buck's face at this unexpected respite from Mr Doyle's criticism. He made good use of it to grab Dusty by the head-collar and turn her to face the gate.

'Listen Buck, I'll call around after tea and treat the thrush myself. It can't be left. The pony is in pain. Anyone with half an eye can see that by the tucked-up look on her. Muck out the shed and have a kettle of boiling water ready for me.'

Buck limped slowly out through the gate without a word. When he was half-way down Braithwaite Street, he gave Dusty a few lashes of the whip to relieve his frustration. There was only one person in the world he had any regard for and that was Danny Doyle and there was only one thing that came between them and that was Dusty.

Kate wasn't at all pleased with the way things had gone. She couldn't help feeling that her father was too soft on Buck. It was always the same. No matter what trouble Buck got himself into, her da was always the one to come to his defence.

'What was all that shouting for?' enquired Mrs Doyle as she poured out the tea. 'I hope you youngsters weren't giving Buck any trouble. That unfortunate man has enough to contend with as it is.' She looked meaningfully at Jamie.

'It wasn't us, ma,' Jamie mumbled through a mouthful of bread and jam, 'it was Buck. He's not looking after Dusty properly. She has thrush and da was giving out to him. And only for Nipper, we wouldn't have known a thing about it. He's better than any bloodhound, so he is.'

'And Buck said he's thinking of selling Dusty to Keefe's the Knackers or to the Pony Express,' Kate added dejectedly. She sat with her elbows on the table, her chin resting in her hands, too upset to eat.

'Well that's the best I've heard in a long time,' said Mrs Doyle with a laugh. 'Buck sell Dusty. What'll he be thinking of next?'

'It's no laughing matter, ma,' said Kate, annoyed

that her mother wasn't taking it seriously. She turned to her father for support but he seemed preoccupied with his thoughts.

'Now Kate,' said Mrs Doyle in a sympathetic tone, 'you know very well that when Buck is drunk he says more than his prayers. Sure, how would he earn his living without Dusty — she's the man's bread and butter, for goodness sake. Now, you'd better drink that sup of tea before it goes stone cold.'

It seemed to Kate that there was no easy answer to Dusty's predicament. If Buck sold her to the Pony Express she would die and if he kept her she would continue to suffer, in which case her life wouldn't be worth living anyway. She wished she could do something but it was all too complicated.

Her father's voice broke in on her thoughts. 'Kate, as soon as you've finished your tea, I want you to yoke Amber to the small cart. I'm going to bring some clean straw around to Buck's. You'd better come with me 'cause I'll need your help. And Jamie, I want you to find an old sock — one without a hole. Fill it with garden lime — it's in the shed — and bring me out the hoof pick as well.'

Within a short time, Kate and her father were on their way around to the Green Yard where Buck lived. As they approached the archway at the entrance, Kate remarked on the number of times Buck had chased herself and her friends out of the laneway.

'All the kids are afraid of him. They call him Dracula because of his big boot and the way he goes on. How is it you and ma don't dislike him the way other people do? I think he's horrible, especially because of the way he treats Dusty.'

Her father sighed heavily and shook his head from side to side several times before answering. 'I know it's impossible to put old heads on young shoulders but I wish you kids would let Buck alone. He's had a hard life, what with the accident and losing all his family when he was a child. People who give out about him don't know him the way your mother and I do. We grew up with him and understand what made him the way he is.'

'But I don't understand, da. If he has had such a hard life why does he make Dusty's life hard too?'

'Because he has a chip on his shoulder. You see, one day, when Buck was only seven, he was scuttin' on the back of a float and a kid from another gang shouted 'scut the whip' to the driver. The driver turned around and lashed the whip at Buck's hands. Buck let go and fell off. Unfortunately, there was another horse and cart galloping along behind. The horse couldn't avoid trampling him and the wheels of the cart went over his foot as well. That's why he wears the big boot. Ever since he has a spite against all horses.'

'But that's stupid, 'said Kate. 'That happened years and years ago and it wasn't the horse's fault.'

'Twenty-eight, to be exact. But that's not the whole story. He spent two years in Steeven's Hospital and during that time both his parents died of TB. His brothers and sisters were put into orphanages and only for his granny and the neighbours, that's where he would've ended up as well. After his granny died he lived with us for three years; that's how we know each other so well.

They both fell silent as they turned the corner at the top of the lane into Redmond's Cottages. Kate couldn't help feeling sorry for Buck but that didn't lessen her dislike for him. Anyway, right now her greatest concern was for Dusty and nothing her parents could say would convince her that Buck didn't intend selling her to the Pony Express.

Suddenly she remembered the leaflets Ned Coyne had given her to deliver that afternoon. She hadn't told her father how she had got on; Dusty's infection had put it clean out of her head. As she began to tell him about all the people who had promised to take part in the protest parade, her spirits rose. Her father looked at her proudly. 'Well now, Kate, that was a great day's work altogether, and tomorrow afternoon there'll be an opportunity for you to do more. In the big shed behind the forge, some people are meeting to make banners and posters for the parade. When I told Ned that you were a dab hand with the drawing, he said for you to come along with your crayons.'

Kate jumped down off the cart feeling a lot happier. The campaign and the coming protest parade filled her with great hope and excitement. Ned Coyne was doing something to stop the Pony Express and he had asked her to help. Her father would nurse Dusty back to health and bring Buck to his senses. Everything would work out right in the end.

They pulled up outside Buck's dilapidated cottage, which was at the end of a row of six. A damaged corrugated gate at the side led into the yard. Buck had just finished mucking out a lean-to shed which served as a stable for Dusty and the yard looked like a slurry pit. Kate's nose twitched at the smell. It was almost as bad as Keefe's the Knackers.

Dusty was tethered to a nail in the wall outside the gate. Kate picked out the mare's hooves then, with a bowl of clean hot water, her father washed Dusty's feet. After each tubbing, Kate lightly tapped each hoof with the lime sock to keep it dry and slightly antiseptic.

'She'll have to have this done several times a day,' Mr Doyle informed Buck, who watched in sullen silence. 'And she can't be worked until the thrush is gone. After that she'll have to have new shoes.'

On Saturday evening Mrs Doyle continued to potter about the kitchen, coming over to the table every now and again to pour tea for someone or to slice bread. She never sat down to eat with the rest, preferring to wait until all were fed before attending to herself.

At one side of the table Whacker and Jamie were enjoying a private joke when all of a sudden Whacker let out a shriek of terror and fell off the chair. Jamie nearly choked himself laughing.

'What in heaven's name are you two up to,' reprimanded Mrs Doyle. 'Give over that horseplay at the table, Whacker, or you'll get no more to eat.' She picked him up off the floor and gave him a good shaking.

'I wasn't doing anything, ma. It was Jamie. He made a bite at my neck, pretending he was Buck and that he was going to suck my blood. I got an awful fright.'

'What do you mean, pretending he was Buck?' enquired his father sharply.

'All the kids call Buck Dracula because he looks like him,' said Whacker innocently.

There was a sudden rush of footsteps outside in the yard, accompanied by wild whoops and shouts. Three heads looked in over the half-door. 'Are you coming out to play, Jamie?' a voice yelled. 'Bobo said we could help him clean out the pigeon lofts if we hurry up. Are you on?'

Jamie looked pleadingly at his father. 'Is it OK, da? Bobo has a new beller and I want to see it.'

'You can.'

Mr Doyle turned to Mrs Doyle. 'Madge, can you spare Kate for about an hour? I'll need her help with Dusty again.'

Kate was delighted to be relieved of her usual Saturday evening chore of having to wash the younger children in the aluminium bath. She was also happy to have the opportunity to talk to her father about Dusty's fate.

Four

On Sunday afternoon, Kate set off for Ned Coyne's forge armed with pencils and crayons. On the way she called for Lila who agreed to come just for the fun of it and because there was nothing else to do.

Unlike Kate, Lila had no interest whatsoever in horses — in fact, she was terrified of them. All she ever wanted to do was sing.

Everyone who heard her agreed she had a fine voice; a second Vera Lynn, they said. The two friends were as different as chalk and cheese. Kate was tall and red-haired, Lila was small and dark. Kate was the eldest of four children, Lila the youngest of fifteen. They were inseparable friends.

When they reached the yard behind the forge they found a few of the neighbours already at work making placards and banners. Jack Foy, the local signwriter, had just finished painting in red letters on a large white banner, 'Export on the HOOK and not on the HOOF.' The slogan made Kate feel slightly uneasy. Before she could question Jack, Mr Coyne caught sight of her and led her across into the shed.

'Watch your step now, girls — it's like a bombsite here at the moment. It's bad enough at the best of times but with all this preparation for the parade there's ten times more rubbish than usual knocking around.'

Very carefully they picked their way over iron bars, fancy wrought-iron gates, window-guards, bits of wood, cart wheels, chains and all manner of forge equipment. Inside the shed, four women and two small girls were seated around a long deal table which was strewn with coloured crêpe paper and rolls of streamers. Kate and Lila were greeted enthusiastically and room was made for them at the table.

'Not so fast,' said Mr Coyne good-humouredly. 'I have other plans for you, Kate. Come over here to this table in the corner where you'll have more elbow-room. Now then, here's the paper and there's the picture. I want you to draw me the head of that horse, nice and big now, so that it fills the top half of the paper, leaving the other half for the slogan. Do you think you could manage that?'

Kate could feel a strange fluttering in her stomach as she looked at the picture. She had seen it before, hanging on the wall in the Coynes' parlour and now fervently wished that her father hadn't boasted about her talent at drawing. Sensing her apprehension, Mr Coyne gave her a friendly pat on the shoulder. 'Don't look so worried, Kate — I'm not expecting a work of art. Just do the best you can.'

Kate propped the picture up against the wall in front of her and began drawing. She was so nervous her hands were shaking. Lila made her worse by hopping over every few minutes to see how she was getting on and giving her advice. When the first head was finished, Lila let out a wild screech.

'That's more like the head of a goat than the head of a horse,' she exclaimed hysterically. Kate felt like killing her, especially when everyone crowded around to share the joke. Someone else said it was the image of Buck Fowler. The tears were running down people's cheeks as names of various animals and local characters were mentioned until in the end Kate ended up laughing herself. From then on her nerves calmed down and her drawings began to improve.

She had six heads finished when Mrs Coyne called from the back door that tea and hot buttered scones were ready on the table. A great cheer went up as everyone downed tools and trooped over towards the kitchen.

'Any news of Mickey Mulligan's cob?' asked Mrs Coyle as she handed round the scones.

'Ne'er a whisper,' replied Kit Lane, who worked as a drayman in Guinness's. 'I met him this morning coming from Mass and the poor man is only demented. He was telling me that the gardai are investigating a amount of similar cases. It seems that there's any number of horses and donkeys missing from different parts of the city — not, indeed, that that's any consolation to Mickey.'

Old Nick Saunders, a saddler from Smithfield, stopped sucking his tea from his saucer to remark, 'Horse-raiding! Did you ever hear the like in all your born life? This country is going to the dogs altogether. Be heavens, it's getting as bad as America.'

'There's no doubt about it but we're living in quare times,' said Tilly Winters, crossing herself. 'God between us and all harm but if things go on as they are, we'll be having to lock our doors at night.'

Everyone laughed at the idea that such drastic action might have to be taken. 'Will you go off outa that,' said Boney Cramer, who reared pigs in a nearby yard. 'Sure half of us haven't got locks, and of them that have, half of them haven't got keys.'

Kitty Dodd looked worried. 'Well, I'm taking no chances, anyway,' she announced. 'Ever since Mickey's cob disappeared, I've been making sure that my mare is barred and bolted in every night. I don't want her ending up in a French stew.' A look of disgust came over her face at the thought. 'Them foreigners are very strange people — they'd eat anything.'

Lila nearly choked laughing and had to pretend that a piece of scone had gone down the wrong way. She whispered into Kate's ear, 'She's a right one to talk. I saw her in Fay's the other day buying cow-heel and tripe. Yuck.'

'Right enough, the rumour is that Mr Big is behind all this stealing,' said Mr Coyne, 'but how to prove it is another thing. The man's a proper gangster. He openly boasts that he can make a thousand pounds a week clear profit on the Pony Express, without doing a hand's turn. Imagine that!'

'I believe that one of his scouts offered Billy Burn fifty pounds for his jennet only last week,' said Mrs Coyne, with a laugh, 'and I wouldn't mind but it's not worth fifty shillings, never mind fifty pounds.'

Kit Lane stopped sucking the stem of his pipe and spoke slowly and deliberately like a man who knew exactly what he was talking about. His eyes swept the room. 'Let me tell you, there's a lot more to this horse-trade than meets the eye. Mr Big isn't the only one making a fortune out of it. What about the men in the beef trade and their friends in the Dáil? They're the very buckos who are kicking up rough against the idea of an Irish horsemeat canning-factory because they say it will endanger the sale of Irish beef abroad.'

'Now you're talking,' agreed Mr Coyne. 'This government is being very short-sighted. Just think of all the jobs a horsemeat factory would bring, not only with canning but also with the by-products — hides, bones, hooves and casings. Sure the country could make thousands on those alone.'

Kate couldn't believe her ears! Surely Mr Coyne wasn't saying that the horses should be killed here and then exported in cans? It just didn't make sense. Did he or did he not want to stop the Pony Express? Then she remembered the slogan Jack Foy had painted on the banner. Mr Lane was right. There was more to this than met the eye.

From then on the conversation became even more complicated for Kate. She heard words that meant absolutely nothing to her and she was too shy and nervous to ask Mr Coyne to explain. Besides, she knew better than to interrupt the conversation.

Later on, Mr Coyne came in to see how she had got on and expressed his delight at the lovely heads she had drawn. 'They're smashing, Kate. Michelangelo couldn't have done better. Now, in your best hand, write in these slogans.' He placed a sheet of paper on the table and Kate read:

STOP Shipping Faithful IRISH HORSES
For CRUEL SLAUGHTER in CONTINENTAL
ABATTOIRS.
SAVE The HORSES That SAVED The HARVEST.
STOP THE IRISH PONY EXPRESS NOW.

Before everyone departed, Mr Coyne announced that a final meeting would be held on the following Friday but in the meantime every effort was to be made to get as many people as possible to join the protest parade on Saturday.

On the way home, Lila was in great form. She had enjoyed herself immensely. Looking at her, Kate couldn't help envying her friend's carefree attitude to life. She was always in good humour. Even the nuns in school had nicknamed her 'Smiler'. No sooner had school entered Kate's mind than she remembered that the summer holidays were almost upon them. As if by magic, her depression evaporated.

'Ay, guess what, Lila. There's only one more week's school before the holliers. Isn't it great?'

Lila threw her arms up in the air. 'Yippee — and do you know what, Kate? I won't be going back after the holliers because I'll be fourteen at the end of August and me ma says I'm to get a job. Just think. No more school eckers or having to face that oul slave-driver with the leather strap. Oh, I just can't wait to be free.' She grabbed hold of Kate and twirled her round and round until they were both dizzy.

Kate was flabbergasted at the news. For ten years she had walked to and from school with Lila, and now, suddenly, this was about to end. In the past, whenever the subject had come up, they had automatically assumed they would both leave school at the same time. The six months difference in their ages had never been taken into account, nor the fact that Lila's widowed mother couldn't wait to get her daughter out to earn her keep. Kate put her hand on the wall and succeeded in steadying her body, but her mind was in a whirl.

'What's the matter, Kate? You look as though you've seen a ghost.'

When Kate opened her mouth to speak, she was surprised that her voice sounded normal. 'But that means we won't be able to see each other every day any more. Even when I come home from school, you'll still be in work.'

'Don't be ridiculous,' replied Lila, giving Kate a nudge with her elbow. 'Won't I be able to see you after work every evening? You'd think I was emigrating to London to hear you talk. Anyway, I haven't got a job yet, but me ma is going to ask Biddy Kershaw to speak for me in her place. She's in a shirt factory in Bonham Street.'

They parted company at Lila's hall door. Kate couldn't help feeling slighted at Lila's apparent indifference to the effect her leaving school would have on their friendship. It was as if she just didn't care. Deep down, Kate knew that when Lila got a job, nothing would ever be the same again. She would start going to the pictures and dances with girls from work, wearing make-up, and before long, start knocking around with fellas. She had seen it happen before between other friends.

Instead of going straight home, she decided to walk up to the canal. She was in no mood to talk and her father would want to know all about the meeting in the forge. The streets around the brewery and the canal basin were quiet now; everybody was in having their tea. For a while she stood watching two swans and three cygnets gliding gracefully up towards the 'gut' and under the iron bridge. The peace and harmony of the scene only served to heighten the desolation and confusion she felt within.

Reflecting on the events of the previous few days, she came to the conclusion that everything had suddenly become very complicated. What with discovering the cruelty to the donkeys, the horrors of the Pony Express, Dusty's thrush and Buck's threat, the Pony Express campaign and now Lila's bombshell about leaving school, it seemed as though a lifetime had been squashed into one weekend. It was far too much for her to cope with all at once.

Her brain was in a whirl as she turned into Newport Street. Scarcely had she rounded the corner when she came to a sudden halt. Tethered by a rope to a lamp-post outside Johnny Power's pub was Dusty! For a moment Kate stood transfixed, thinking she was seeing things. But there was no mistake. Buck had broken his promise — again.

Carefully, Kate pushed opened the pub door and peeped in. There was Buck, sitting over at the wall, drinking with two strange men. One of them took something out of his pocket and slipped it across the table to Buck. It was money. Buck looked up, his usually dour face creased into a satisfied grin. She drew back quickly before he could see her. At first she was at a loss what to do, then suddenly, all was clear. She turned from the door, went straight over to Dusty, unwound the rope and led the mare slowly homeward.

Five

At no stage did Kate stop to consider the effect the mare's disappearance would have on Buck. As far as she was concerned he wanted Dusty only to take him back home safely after closing time. The fact that the mare wasn't yoked up to the cart didn't strike her as odd, nor did it cross her mind that Buck wouldn't be able to leap up on the mare's back. Neither did she attach any significance to the exchange of money between the stranger and Buck. Right now, her mind was totally concentrated on Dusty's welfare.

The family was seated around the table having tea when she ran in the door. Before her mother had time to complain about her being late, Kate launched into her story about Dusty. As she had anticipated, her father was furious at Buck's negligence but he wasn't at all pleased that she had taken Dusty without Buck's knowledge or permission.

'But what could I do, da? He was with these strange men and he was drunk. You know I'm terrified of him, especially when he's like that. And I saw one of the men slipping him a bundle of notes so I guessed he was going to be drinking for a long time.'

This last piece of news had an electrifying effect on

her father. He banged his cup down, spilling the tea all over the saucer, scraped his chair back from the table and rushed over to the door for his jacket.

'Merciful heavens, Danny, will you take it easy,' cried Mrs Doyle in alarm. 'There's no need to upend the place. Look at the mess you're after making all over the table.' She clicked her tongue in annoyance.

Mr Doyle appeared not to hear, as he struggled with his jacket sleeves. 'Quick, Kate,' he urged. 'Yoke Amber up to the trap and follow me around to Power's pub. Jamie, look after Dusty. Put down clean straw in the shed and give her water. Whacker, make her up a feed of oats, and Madge, have a big kettle of water boiled by the time I get back.' With that he vanished out the door.

Mrs Doyle heaved a sigh and shook her head. She was about to clear the table when she remembered that Kate hadn't eaten. 'You'd better come back in and have your tea before it's spoiled,' she called to her across the yard. 'God knows I've been keeping it hot long enough and if you don't eat it now it won't be worth eating.'

But food was the last thing on Kate's mind. 'I'll have it when I get back, ma. I won't be long. Leave it on the hob.'

In record time she had Amber between the shafts of the trap and was galloping up Marrowbone Lane to Power's pub. Outside the pub, tethered to a lamp-post, a scrawny pony stood waiting patiently for its owner to emerge. Its head was buried deep inside a sackful of oats hanging from the headband, a sure sign that the owner was going to be inside for some time.

Even before she opened the door Kate could hear the sound of voices raised in anger. In the dim interior she could see that the bar had filled up considerably in the short time since she'd last peeped in. Buck was shouting incoherently and punching the air with his clenched fists while her father had a man by the collar and was shaking him vigorously. It was the man who had given Buck the money. The two other strangers had their arms pinned behind their backs, having been overpowered by the rest of the men in the bar.

Nobody paid any attention to Kate, who stood transfixed inside the door. She had never, ever, seen her father so angry. 'Who sent you here?' he kept demanding, punctuating each word with a shake of the man's body.

The man looked terrified. 'Take it easy, mister, take it easy,' he begged. 'I can explain, if you'll only give me a chance. Just let go my neck before you choke me.'

Mr Doyle shoved him against the wall. The man adjusted his collar and tie and rubbed his neck before speaking. 'We heard from a client that your man here had a mare for sale and we called around to his yard to see if we could clinch a deal. He was interested so we brought him around here for a drink just to give him time to consider, which he did. What's it to you, anyway?'

'Don't give me any of your lip,' warned Mr Doyle, holding up a clenched fist in front of the stranger's face. 'I know your game and who's behind you. You're on the lookout for horses for Mr Big of the

Pony Express, aren't you?'

For a moment there was silence. The man looked fearfully around the bar and licked his lips before replying. 'Look, mister, I don't know what you're talking about. I just want an animal to haul turf from the Phoenix Park to the turf depots around the city. My mates there came along only to keep me company. That's all, I swear.'

'How much did you hand over to Buck?' asked Kate's father.

'Fifty pounds — which is more than the oul nag is worth.'

Just as Mr Doyle was about to turn to Buck for confirmation, there was an almighty crash and the sound of shattering glass. Buck had fallen to the floor and knocked over a table laden with drink. Uproar and confusion followed, as efforts were made to help him to his feet. When he was finally settled into a sitting position, Kate's father searched his pockets and produced a bundle of notes rolled up in an elastic band.

'Is this what you gave him?' The man nodded. Mr Doyle stuffed the money into the top pocket of the man's jacket and grabbed him by the shoulder. 'Take your blood-money and get out of here on the double. And you can count yourself lucky that it hasn't cost you your life.'

At a nod from Kate's father, two locals opened the door and the three men were thrown out into the street. Kate had taken refuge in the snug, just in time, but in the mêlée that followed, she slipped outside and ran over to the trap. A few moments later, her father emerged he and a number of other men carrying Buck's lifeless form. Carefully, they lifted him up into the trap and sat him down on the seat, holding him upright until Kate's father got in beside him. One of the men offered to accompany him to Buck's cottage.

'Right you are, Kate,' her father said with a nod. 'Take it nice and easy around to the Green Yard.'

As soon as they arrived, Mr Doyle told Kate to run home. 'Tell your mother I'll be back soon — I just want to get Buck into bed. Get started on Dusty's feet — tell Jamie I said he's to give you a hand.'

Much to Kate's surprise, when she got home Jamie already had Dusty's hooves washed and disinfected. 'I had to do them,' he explained. 'Ma wouldn't let me go around to Duckser's loft to see his new tumblers until they were done. She was giving out about you wasting your time with horses and me wasting my time with pigeons instead of learning something useful. You'll probably get it now, when you go in.'

But her mother only asked about Buck. Kate said nothing about the row inside the pub, only that Buck was very drunk and that they had taken him home. She was munching a cold rasher sandwich when her father returned.

'He'll be all right after a night's sleep. Paddy Miley said he'll stay with him till morning just to make sure. Something will have to be done about him and the drink, though. It's the last straw when he goes the lengths of selling Dusty for fifty pounds to those three go-boys from the Pony Express.' He patted Kate on the shoulder. 'You did a good job there spotting that transaction. Only for you, Dusty would be gone by now.'

Kate was tempted to say she'd told him that Buck couldn't be trusted, but she stopped herself in time. Instead she asked, 'What's going to happen to Dusty now? Buck might try selling her again.'

'I don't think we'll hear anything more from Mr Big's scouts. Not after the shock they got in Power's when all them big, strong dockers from the harbour began to show their muscles.' He laughed heartily as he recalled the frightened look on the strangers' faces. 'As to what will happen to Dusty, well, she can stay here for a few days. I'll make Buck come around and give me a hand.'

'Make sure you do just that,' said Kate's mother tersely. 'I've enough to do here, God knows, and could do with a bit of help from Kate, so don't go taking up her time. Talking about which,' she said, turning to Kate, 'it's time you went to bed or you won't be fit for school tomorrow.'

For the next few days, Buck was on his best behaviour. Mr Doyle continued to look after Dusty's feet but he made sure that Buck did all her feeding and grooming. By Wednesday there was a decided improvement in the mare's appearance. The knots and tangles in her mane and tail had been removed and her coat began to take on a shine. So that Buck wouldn't be at any financial loss, Mr Doyle let him have a loan of Amber for a few hours every day with a strict warning not to use a whip or chafe the sides of her mouth with excessive chucking of the reins.

At midday on Friday, the school holidays began and Kate and Lila walked out the gate together for the last time. Lila threw her schoolbag into the air, shouting, 'I'm free, I'm free.' She was joined by three others from sixth class who had also finished school and the four of them formed a circle around their schoolbags, whirling and yelling madly until they collapsed in an exhausted heap on the footpath.

Along with everyone else, Kate was caught up in the euphoria of the occasion. Two months of summer holidays lay ahead and as well as that, she was looking forward to the parade tomorrow. It wasn't until they were finally alone at the top of the Coombe that she remembered that this was it — their last walk home from school together.

Lila was too excited to notice Kate's silence. She rattled on about the interview she was having for the shirt factory on the following Monday and asked Kate to keep her fingers crossed that she would get the job. Kate promised, and in turn asked Lila not to forget the parade next day. They parted casually but by the time she reached the corner of Summer Street, Kate was ready to burst into tears.

The minute she entered the yard she sensed that something was wrong. A number of neighbours were crowded round her father, who was unyolking Amber from Buck's scrap-cart. She went straight into the kitchen to find out from her mother what was wrong and found her bending over a figure lying on the old sofa against the wall.

'Lie there quietly for a while, Buck,' she was saying as she tucked a blanket round him, 'and in no time at all you'll be as right as rain. I'll make you a nice cup of tea now and you just close your eyes and relax.'

'What's the matter, ma?'

Mrs Doyle put her finger to her lips and took Kate aside. 'There's been a terrible accident below on Winetavern Street hill,' she whispered. 'Buck was nearly killed by a runaway horse. Your father will tell you all about it while I'm making the tea.'

When Kate emerged, the neighbours had departed and Mr Doyle was throwing a blanket over Amber. She could see by the tense expression on his face that he was very worried.

'Is Amber all right?' she asked anxiously. 'Ma said something about a runaway horse.'

'Amber is game-ball, just a bit uptight. Will you tether her over here by the shed so that she'll be near Dusty. That'll settle her. Buck is the one I'm worried about. It's the mercy of God that he wasn't killed or injured. As it is, he's very badly bruised and shocked, which is serious enough.' He shook his head slowly from side to side. 'I don't know what it is at all, but there's a jinx on that man with horses.'

Kate had never seen Amber so agitated. She kept flicking her ears and dilating her nostrils. Every now and again she snorted loudly as though she were trying to express her feelings. Dusty seemed to understand. She whinnied softly and gave Amber a face-lick.

'And what happened to the runaway horse?' asked Kate. Her father was trying to move Buck's scrap-cart over to the wall. He stopped and took in a deep breath.

'That's the most unpleasant part of the story. Give us a hand with this first, then I'll tell you all about it.'

Six

'From what I can gather,' said Kate's father, pushing the peak of his cap back off his forehead, 'Buck had just rounded the corner of Wood Quay, and was leading Amber up the hill, when he heard these roars and screams and saw people scattering in all directions. Down the hill came the clatter of hooves and he sees this big Clydesdale stallion, wild-eyed and foaming at the mouth, making for him. As it came alongside him, he made a grab at the halter-rope around its neck in the hopes of slowing it down but didn't it rear up on its hind legs and lifted him several feet into the air. He hit the ground with an almighty wallop and was dragged several yards before he let go. The horse must've been blind with fear because it just kept on galloping out onto the quays and made straight for the Liffey wall and jumped.'

'My God!' exclaimed Kate. 'Is it ...?' She couldn't bring herself to say it.

Mr Doyle paused a moment before answering. Then in a voice filled with sadness he said, 'Unfortunately, the tide was out and the poor animal was so badly injured it had to be shot.'

Kate's eyes opened wide in horror and she clasped

her hands over her mouth to stifle a scream. She had seen runaway horses before and was well aware of the terror they created in a crowded street but the manner in which the stallion had met his death shocked her so much that she had to sit down on the shaft of Buck's cart.

'I'm sorry, Kate, to be so blunt, but there's no way I can dress the truth up to make it more palatable.'

Kate said nothing. She seemed dazed. Her father was about to say something else, but hesitated and instead bent down and picked up an empty bucket and began filling it under the yard tap. The splashing sound of the water brought Kate back to life.

'Why did the horse run wild in the first place?' she asked in a low voice. 'Something must've happened to it.'

'Well, there were plenty of witnesses to what happened. It seems that the horse was limping badly because one of its shoes was missing. At the top of the hill it refused to budge another inch and the guy leading it whipped it unmercifully. The poor thing went berserk. The guy tried to bring it under control but the horse lashed out with its hind legs and sent him sprawling.'

Kate stood up and went over to Amber who was now happily slurping the water in the bucket. 'Well, I'm glad the horse didn't let him away with it. After all, only for him it would be alive now.'

Mr Doyle was bent over, examining Dusty's hoof. He straightened himself up slowly and gave Kate a long, earnest look. 'I hate having to say it, but the poor animal is better off dead. You see, it was on its way from Wicklow to the Pony Express.'

A wave of anger surged through Kate's body at this last piece of information. 'I hate that Pony Express,' she cried. 'No matter what way you look at it, it has caused the horse's death. Oh, da, why can't we stop it? And to think that poor Dusty only barely escaped.' Overcome with emotion she ran over to the mare and threw her arms around its neck. Suddenly, all her pent-up feelings of the past week dissolved into a flood of tears.

Her father didn't know what to do. It wasn't like Kate to break down and cry. She was always so sensible. He searched in his pocket for a handkerchief and at the same time took out his pipe.

'Here, dry your eyes or you'll only upset your mother,' was all he could think of saying.

Feeling foolish at her outburst, Kate blew her nose and wiped her eyes. After a few shivery sobs, she asked in a nasally voice, 'How did Amber get back if Buck was hurt?'

'Easy,' replied her father, relieved that she was her old self once more. 'A few fellas recognised him and made a place for him in among the scrap. Then one of them drove him home. Your mother dressed all his cuts and scratches but if he isn't well tomorrow morning we'll have to get the dispensary doctor. Such a time for all this to happen and I up to my eyes preparing for the parade, and Dusty out of action as well.'

'You don't have to worry about Dusty,' said Kate, giving the mare's nose an affectionate rub. 'I'll take care of her. I'm on holidays now.'

Mr Doyle's face lit up. 'You know, I clean forgot about that. Between yourself and Jamie I should be able to manage well enough. I'd better get a move on now. The trap has to be varnished for the parade and then there's the final meeting tonight in Ned Coyne's.' He turned to her as they crossed the yard. 'Smile, for God's sake, and don't let your mother know you were crying or I'll never hear the end of it.'

Buck was sitting up, drinking a cup of tea, when they entered the cottage. The legs of his trousers were torn to shreds and both his hands and legs were swathed in bandages made from strips of white sheets. To Kate, he looked more frightening than ever.

The smell of fried kippers was all over the kitchen. Mrs Doyle was busy buttering a plate of bread. 'You'd better run up to Joe Burdock's for your chips,' she said to Kate, 'and if you see Nora and Whacker, tell them they'd better to come home for their dinner.'

Kate was only too happy to get away from the sight of Buck and the smell of the kippers. As usual on a Friday, the chip-shop was crowded. Everyone was talking about the runaway horse and Buck's attempt to halt it. They all had their own version of the story and although none of them had actually witnessed the incident, they added an extra piece for dramatic effect. It was agreed by one and all that Buck had acted very bravely indeed, without as much as a thought for his own safety. Kate listened in amazement. She had never heard anyone say anything good about Buck before. Now here he was being elevated to the status of local hero.

On the way home, she made a hole in the newspaper wrapping and started picking away at the contents. The familiar salty, vinegary taste of the freshly fried chips had a relaxing and comforting effect on her. She began to question her own attitude to Buck.

Up to now, she hadn't given a thought to his role in the morning's tragic event. After hearing the neighbours' views, she began to realise that he had indeed risked his life and that his action was really praiseworthy when she thought of his past experience with horses and his disability. She felt awful, not only because she had ignored his injuries and pain, but because she had also recoiled at the sight of his pitiful appearance, which, after all, was only the result of his unselfish action. She wished that she could make amends but she didn't know how.

By the time she reached home, Whacker and Nora were already waiting for their chips. Jamie still hadn't returned from school. The first thing Kate noticed was that Buck had changed out of his dirty rags and was wearing some of her father's clothes. The difference these made in his appearance surprised her so much that she kept casting quick glances at him when he wasn't looking just to convince herself that she wasn't imagining things. Then, without any conscious decision to do so, she found herself telling Buck what the people in Burdock's had said about him.

'That's nothing but a load of oul codswallop,' he muttered in his usual dour way. 'A hero is right. I wasn't thinking of anyone or anything but Amber and myself. All I wanted to do was to stop the stallion from crashing into Amber because I was terrified that Danny would take my sacred life if anything happened to her.'

'Will you go on outa that, Buck, and stop selling yourself short,' said Kate's father with a laugh. 'If the people want to believe that you're a hero, let them. Haven't you been derided often enough in the past, so you might as well enjoy the bit of praise now. It's no more than you deserve. What does it matter why you tried to stop the horse? You tried — that's the important thing.'

Buck just nodded his head resignedly and said nothing. Kate couldn't take her eyes off him. His reason for trying to halt the stallion meant more to her than anything else in the world. He had done it to save Amber! It suddenly dawned on her what the consequences might have been if he hadn't. The feeling of horror she had experienced at the death of the stallion took hold of her again, but this time the image was that of Amber lying dead. Fortunately, before her mind could linger too much on the ghastly picture, her mother's voice burst in on her thoughts.

'You'd better clear away the dishes, Kate — I've to finish off Rosie McCann's costume for the wedding and I need the table. Whacker, run into your granny's and see if she wants any messages. Where in the name of fortune has that Jamie fella got himself to? He should be home from school by now.'

Everyone got Mrs Doyle's hint that things had better return to normal. Mr Doyle stood up, adjusted his braces and said to Buck, 'How's the form now? Just say when you want to go home and I'll take you in the trap, but you know you're welcome to lie there as long as you wish.'

Buck elected to go home immediately. He wasn't used to all the attention, and besides, the noise of the younger children playing was getting on his nerves. Kate helped her father yoke Amber up to the trap, then with the aid of both her parents, Buck slowly and painfully climbed inside.

'I'll call around later on with a bite to eat,' promised Kate's mother as they disappeared out the gate. 'I hope he's going to be all right,' she said, turning to Kate. 'He really needs someone to look after him for a few days because he's not going to be able to move about. Now, you'll have to give me a hand with this costume or Rosie'll have a fit. You do the hem while I'm doing the buttonholes.'

Kate sat by the window stitching, and watching enviously as Jamie helped her father put a coat of varnish on the trap. This was Jamie's punishment for having gone to Gabby Moore's pigeon loft instead of coming straight home from school. In vain he pleaded to be allowed go with his friends up to the canal for a swim. Secretly, his father sympathised with him, remembering his own youth when pigeons were all that mattered in life, but he, too, had to learn the hard way.

Kate's mother hummed and chatted as she ran the material through the machine. 'Thanks be to God you got your holidays — I've a ton of stitching to be done. By the way, did Lila hear any word yet about that job in the shirt factory?'

'She's to go for an interview on Monday,' replied Kate, wishing the subject hadn't been brought up.

'That's great news. She won't know herself bringing home a wage-packet although she won't make as much at the shirts as she would at the tailoring. Still, it's a start. Once she learns how to use the machine that's the main thing.'

Kate remained silent. She knew from experience where the conversation was leading and was in no mood to get into an argument. She was saved from any further comment on the topic by the entry of her father.

'Well, that's that job done and I'm not sorry. I only hope to God it doesn't rain on it now. I thought I felt a few splashes a while ago. It would be just like it to pour down with all the praying the farmers are doing after the long dry spell.'

The familiar cry of Curley, the paperman, was heard in the distance. As soon as he entered the yard he roared, 'Stop Press, Stop Press. Read all about it. Horse jumps to death in Liffey horror.' He threw a copy of the *Evening Mail* down on the kitchen table in front of Mr Doyle.

'Inside there are pictures and all of the horse and eye-witness accounts of Buck's attempt to halt it. Everyone's saying that he's lucky to be alive.'

When Curley departed, Mr Doyle opened the paper and the family crowded around. There were two pictures, one with the horse lying below in the Liffey mud, the other showing it being hauled up by a huge crane. The photographs described much better than any words could, how horrible the incident had been. The accompanying report described what had happened and also highlighted the fact that the horse had been on its way to board the 'notorious Pony Express'.

Mr Doyle folded the paper carefully. 'This dreadful occurrence will have to be discussed at the meeting tonight. Who knows but some good may come out of it yet. Tomorrow's protest parade will be the first test so let's hope the people turn out in hordes.'

Seven

The first thing Kate did when she woke up on Saturday morning was to look out the window to check the weather. She was disappointed to find that the sky wasn't as clear as it had been for the previous few days, but it wasn't raining and that was the main thing.

It was still early morning when she finished the major chores about the yard. While disinfecting Dusty's feet, she was delighted to see that the inflamation had all but disappeared and that the pony was in much better spirits.

Reflecting on the unfortunate circumstances that had given Dusty into her care she wondered how long it would take for Buck to recover. A week maybe, or less? Her sympathy for him was tempered by her concern for Dusty. While on the one hand she wished him well, on the other she reasoned that the longer he was out of action, the better it would be for the mare.

She had entertained a fervent hope that her father would buy Dusty. When she had suggested this, he had dismissed it on the grounds that he didn't need two ponies and even if he did, he hadn't the money. 'Anyway, there'd be nothing to stop Buck getting another pony and treating it just as badly,' he had pointed out. 'No, the answer to the problem is to change Buck's attitude, and to do that we must first get him off the drink. In the meantime, I'll just have to be more vigilant.'

As soon as Dusty's grooming was completed, Kate strung a hay-net on the tethering ring outside the shed and left the mare chewing away contentedly. Mrs Doyle emerged from the cottage, carrying a billy-can wrapped in a towel and a paper parcel.

'I'm off around to Buck's with a sup of tea and a few cuts of bread. I shouldn't be gone for more than half an hour. Get the other two out of bed and give them their breakfast and tell Whacker his father said he's to Brasso Amber's medallions.'

Before going indoors Kate removed her wellingtons and washed her feet under the cold running water from the yard tap. She felt so hot and sweaty she wished she could remove all her clothes and hose herself from top to toe. Instead, she had to make do with the usual unsatisfactory neck and face wash in the kitchen sink.

When Mrs Doyle returned she looked worried. 'Buck is hardly able to move he's so sore. Every bit of him is black and blue and one of his legs looks as if it's gone septic, it's that red and swollen. I'm going to take around a bit of flakemeal to make a poultice and you'll have to come with me and give me a hand.'

Kate's heart sank. She dreaded seeing Buck and his septic wounds but there was no use protesting — her mother would make her go no matter what. She had intended running around to see Lila to tell her the latest on the parade. That would have to wait now.

She felt angry and frustrated. All her rushing had been for nothing.

Mrs Doyle told Kate to get a bowl, cotton wool, pieces of old clean sheets, Dettol, lint, scissors and flakemeal, while she filled a flask with boiling water. These were all put into an oil-cloth market bag. In less than ten minutes they were on their way.

It was a long time since Kate had been inside Buck's cottage. She had a vague memory of it being unpleasant, but still she wasn't prepared for the scene of dirt and squalor that met her eyes. The floor was strewn with empty Guinness bottles, dirty tumblers, cigarette butts, spent matches and sacks. Several empty, unrinsed milk bottles stood on the wooden draining board. On a small iron bed, to the side of the fireplace, Buck lay stretched, with his head resting on a greasy, uncovered bolster. One of his injured legs was raised up on a pile of sacks. The only cheerful thing in the room was the red glow from the turf fire that Mrs Doyle had lit earlier on.

Buck turned his face towards them when they entered. His eyes met Kate's and sent a shiver down her spine. Stuck across his nose was a large plaster, and on either side, his face was scratched and bruised. Kate wanted to run.

'Now then, Buck,' said Mrs Doyle cheerfully, 'I'll give the oul leg a bit of a wash first with the Dettol and water before clapping on the poultice. It's looking very angry, God bless it, but once that pus is gone, you'll feel as fit as a fiddle. Here, bring over that towel, Kate, and as soon as I lift up the leg, slip it in underneath.'

Buck never uttered a sound. Gently and deftly, Mrs

Doyle attended to the swollen limb while Kate handed her whatever she needed. After making up the hot poultice, Mrs Doyle spread it quickly between two pieces of lint which she then placed on the bandage. The minute the hot dressing touched the swelling, Buck let out a deafening roar which trailed off into a string of curses, but he never once tried to push Mrs Doyle's hand away. While he was writhing in agony, she kept up a stream of consoling patter until the bandage was securely tied.

Kate was astonished at Buck's submission to such torture. She suddenly thought of Dusty and of the similarity between her condition and his, and wondered if that would occur to him. On impulse, she decided that now would be a golden opportunity to remind him. It might make him realise how cruel he had been to deliberately ignore the mare's infection. Lacking the courage to address him directly she spoke to her mother instead.

'Dusty's feet are nearly better, ma. She'll soon be well enough to get her new shoes. You know, I was just thinking of how funny it is that she and Buck are suffering from infections at the same time. Just imagine, only da treated her in time she'd probably be dead by now.'

The insinuation in Kate's remarks wasn't lost upon her mother, who froze her with one of her deadly, silent stares. Kate didn't care. She was fed up with the way her mother constantly tried to shield Buck from criticism. Someone had to make him realise that if his infection were left untreated, he too could die. She ventured a look to see what effect, if any, her words had on him, but his eyes were closed and he remained silent.

To her relief, as soon as Buck's wounds were washed and dressed, her mother said she could go home. 'Your father'll be back early. I won't be much longer here — I just want to empty the ash and bank up the fire. As soon as you get home, check that the stew is okay.'

Kate raced down the Green Yard. On her way past Furlong's shop she called in for her weekly *Girl's Crystal*, hoping to have a read before her father's return but when she entered the yard, he was already unharnessing Amber.

'Oh, good — you're back. Where's your mother?'

When Kate told him about Buck's septic leg he sighed. 'I suppose I ought to pay him a visit. It might need to be treated by the dispensary doctor. An infection like that could be very serious for him.' Just as he was on the point of departing Mrs Doyle appeared, all hot and flushed from rushing.

'There's no need for you to go around to him now,' she assured him.' He knows you're up to your eyes with the parade as well as everything else. Anyway, there's no call for any worry. He'll be game-ball. Just leave him to me — I know what I'm doing.' She made straight for the kitchen to check on the stew. Satisfied, she brushed the stray strands of hair back off her forehead. 'Now, come on, sit down and eat — you must be exhausted.'

Immediately after dinner, Kate began grooming Amber for the parade. By the time she was finished, the pony looked as though she was bound for the Dublin Horse Show. Her chestnut coat shone like burnished gold and her hooves were cleaned and oiled. For added effect, Kate had arranged her beautiful, long, black mane into seven pigtails and formed each one into a small tight knot at the root. All that remained now was to put on her polished harness and brass medallions before bringing her out into the yard for inspection.

Mr Doyle had to admit that he had never seen Amber look so lovely. 'She's more like a thoroughbred than a cart-horse. And will you look at the way she's tossing her head and swishing her tail as if she knew she was all dolled up.' He took his watch out of his waistcoat pocket. 'Good God,' he exclaimed, 'is that the time? You'd better run along now and get yourself ready or we'll be late.'

The parade was due to start at three o'clock from St Stephen's Green. The previous night, at the meeting in Ned Coyne's, the placards and posters had been distributed.

'You'll be happy to know,' Ned had announced proudly, 'that the champion jockey, Aubrey Brabazon will be leading the parade and he'll be flanked by Captain Ian Dudgeon, the famous showjumper and Major Kulesza, the trainer of the Irish jumping team. The Dublin Society for the Prevention of Cruelty to Animals is expecting a huge turnout so I suggest we meet outside the Russell Hotel and parade together as a group.'

Kate was beginning to get worried about Lila's non-appearance. With only minutes to spare before they were due to depart, she came rushing breathlessly into the yard. Kate heaved a sigh of relief. 'It's about time. I thought we'd have to go without you. Come on, jump up.'

Lila was holding her side and gasping. 'Oh, Kate,

I'm sorry but I can't come. I've to go to see Biddy
Kershaw to get the low-down on what to say at the
interview on Monday. I hope you don't mind, but
you know how it is.'

The smile disappeared from Kate's face. She stared
at Lila in disbelief. 'No Lila, I don't know how it is.
You promised me faithfully that you'd come today
and now here you are dashing off somewhere else.
Why can't you go to see Biddy later on? She isn't
going to run away, is she?'

Lila looked uncomfortable. 'Look, I know I
promised, but honest to God, I can't do anything
about it. It's me ma. She's making me go now and
she's coming along with me. I'm really sorry, Kate.
Tell you what. I'll call around after tea and you can let
me know how things went. I'll have to go now or my
life won't be worth living. S'long.' With a wave she
was gone.

Kate was so disappointed she didn't answer. She
had really been looking forward to Lila's company for
the parade. It certainly wasn't going to be as
enjoyable without her. She tried to hide her feelings
as she stepped up into the trap and took the reins
from her father.

'I take it that Lila isn't coming after all,' he
observed. 'You do the driving and I'll keep an eye on
these two. Jamie, you sit on the far side and hold that
poster of the horse's head straight up so that it can be
seen. Right, Kate, hit the road.'

Kate flicked the reins and clicked her tongue.
Amber obediently moved forward. 'Enjoy yourselves,' shouted Mrs Doyle, giving a wave as they
turned out the gate. At the top of the Coombe, the

filly broke into a canter. Neighbours out doing their Saturday afternoon shopping saluted Danny gaily while the young people gazed enviously at Kate sitting in the driver's seat.

When they reached Cuffe Street, Kate reduced Amber's speed to a slow trot. Horses of every description seemed to be converging on Stephen's Green. Lila's desertion was temporarily forgotten. Kate's spirits rose. She couldn't believe that so many people were supporting the protest. It was getting more difficult to drive Amber through the crowds, so Mr Doyle got down and led her forward.

'Over here, Kate,' a voice called above the clamour. Waving at her from the seat of a cab was Ned Coyne. Kate and her father manoeuvred Amber across towards the railings where there was a long line of horses and vehicles. A great cheer went up from the crowd at the sight of the beautiful pony and trap.

'Right, everybody,' Ned roared. 'Follow Kate to join the main body on the other side of the Green.'

Kate could feel her heart thumping madly with excitement as the steward directed her in behind a large group of marchers representing the various organisations associated with the protest. In the distance could be heard the wails and screeches of the pipe bands tuning up.

'Oh da, isn't it great? The whole world is here.'

'Don't get too carried away. Most of these people are only here out of curiosity. They probably don't even know what it's all about. When the parade begins you'll get a better picture of what real support we have.'

Jamie was standing up, giving a running commentary on what was happening up front. 'Janey Mac, da, you should see it — it's only massive. There's another pipe band right up the front and there's loads of people in riding suits on racehorses and people waving green-white-and-orange flags. Oh, I think it's starting — your man leading the first band is after throwing his stick up into the sky. Look, it's twiddling round and round in the air. I'd laugh if he misses it on the way down. Jaypers! He's after catching it!' Jamie's mouth hung open in amazement.

'Don't be too quick off the mark now, Kate,' her father advised. 'Give that group in front a good cart-length before you start.'

The deep, dull, boom of the big, bass drum signalled the pipers to begin. As the first discordant notes of the bagpipes filled the air, the parade staggered and shuffled into life. Kate took a quick glance behind to indicate to Nick Saunders, the saddler, that she was about to move off. Her heart nearly burst with pride at the sight of all the familiar horses and neighbours waiting at the ready for her signal. Then, with cheers and waves from the crowd, the first Pony Express Protest Parade began its journey through the city's centre to the martial strains of 'Let Erin Remember'.

Eight

True to her promise, Lila called around after tea, by which time Kate's good humour had returned. The success of the protest parade was undoubtedly a contributory factor but she had also had plenty of time to reflect on Lila's reason for not attending the parade.

Lila's father was dead and her mother was mentally and physically exhausted trying to raise her large family on the widow's pension and charity. Getting the job in the shirt factory was more important to Lila than anything else in the world right now. Deep down, Kate knew that Lila would have preferred to have been at the parade. The music and excitement would have appealed to her fun-loving nature. Kate had to admit that she had been selfish in thinking only of her own disappointment, when in actual fact, Lila was the one who had lost out.

'Oh, I wish you'd been there, Lila.' Kate's face lit up as she described the excitement of it all. 'You'd have loved it. I'll never forget the crowds all lined along the streets, cheering and shouting, and just as we got near to Parnell's Monument we saw the beginning of the parade coming down the other side of O'Connell's Street. There were all these beautiful racehorses with riders dressed up in riding outfits and behind them was a pipe band and more people marching with flags and banners.'

The two friends were sitting on a low window-sill in the Doyles' yard. Inside in the kitchen, Whacker and Nora were noisily enjoying their regular Saturday night bath in front of the fire. When Kate heard her mother threatening them to a good slap if they didn't stop dousing the floor, she decided it was time to make herself scarce.

'If we hang around here much longer, I'll be called in to help. Come on and we'll go for a walk up Thomas Street and look at the shop windows. I'll tell you the rest about the parade on the way.' They slipped out through the wicket-gate and with arms linked together they made off quickly down the street before Kate's mother had time to notice her disappearance.

'We paraded all the way back to Foster Place,' Kate continued, 'then all these people got up on a dray and made speeches. Some of them had travelled on the Pony Express themselves, just to see what it was like, so they had first hand information. It was hard to hear what they were saying most of the time because there was nothing but booing and cheering and every now and again a boxing match broke out. In the end, me da got so nervous he decided we'd better go home.'

'Well, at least you had a bit of fun, whereas I was only fit to be tied, listening to me ma and Biddy Kershaw. You should've heard them. They went on and on about what it was like in their day, as if things were any better now. Then Biddy gives me this rigmarole on how I'm to behave at the interview. I'm to say 'pardon' instead of 'what' and I'm not to forget to say 'sir' and 'mam' to the boss and forewoman every time they ask me a question. Did ever you hear the like?' She gave Kate a playful push against the wall. 'I only hope to God I don't burst out laughing.'

'What time is the interview?' asked Kate after she had recovered her balance.

'Well, I've to be there at nine o'clock in the morning — that's when work usually begins, but Biddy said I might have to hang around waiting for the boss because he doesn't come in sometimes until ten o'clock. She said he's a demon and that he treats all the girls like dirt. By the time she was finished I was sorry I'd ever heard about the job.'

Sauntering along arm-in-arm, they moved from shop to shop, wishing their hearts out for the styles on view. Lila squashed her nose against McDonnell's window, her eyes filled with longing. 'Just think, Kate, if I get this job I'll be able to join a clothes' club and buy myself something nice, instead of having to make do with hand-me-downs and second-hand shoes from the Iveagh. You know, I've never, ever, had a single thing bought just for me.'

Kate gave Lila's arm a gentle squeeze but said nothing. She knew Lila wasn't looking for sympathy, just making a statement of fact. Returning home by Meath Street, they met friends from school who were also out window-shopping. For a while all cares and woes were forgotten. A clock chimed somewhere in the distance and Kate suddenly remembered she had left the yard without permission.

'Holy cow,' she exclaimed. 'There's nine o'clock

ringing out. I'll be killed, so I will. Quick Lila, come on — I'll have to run.'

By the time they reached Lila's hall door, they were completely out of breath. 'I'll call for you in the morning on the way to Mass,' Kate gasped without stopping. She burst in through the cottage door all prepared for her mother's attack, only to find her granny seated alone by the window darning socks.

'Is the divil after you or what?' Granny Doyle enquired, looking up over the top of her spectacles.

Kate's eyes anxiously searched the room. 'Hello, gran. Where's ma?'

'She went around to Buck's after your father. The rest are in bed this half hour. Your mother left that bit of ironing there for you to do, so you'd better get it done before she gets back. And is it any harm to ask, but where were you gallivanting to at this hour of the night?'

'Was ma giving out? I was only leaving Lila home and we were just chatting. I never felt the time passing.'

'Leaving Lila home is right,' said granny with a sly grin. 'A little bird told me that you were seen falling around Meath Street laughing along with a bevy of young rossies.'

Kate blushed at being found out telling a lie. Granny gave a little chuckle. Putting down her work, she stuck her hand in the pocket of her cross-over bib and produced her snuff-box. Opening it up, she dipped in her finger and thumb, gently tapped off the surplus, then loudly sniffed a pinch up each nostril.

'I don't think your mother noticed you were gone,' she said, giving her upper lip a quick wipe with the back of her hand. 'Meself and your granda popped in to see how Buck was getting on and she said she was just about to go around to dress his leg, so I offered to put the childer to bed.'

'Thanks, gran. You're an angel for not squealing on me.'

'Ah, sure I was young meself once, Kate. Now then, I think I'd better go in next door or your granda'll think I've run off with a sailor.' Granny hoisted herself up out of the chair with difficulty and shuffled slowly towards the door. 'Tell your mother all them socks is mended. Goodnight, Kate. Sleep well.'

Kate woke to the clangorous peal of Sunday church bells. She lay listening for a while, sorting out the various tones and rhythms, easily recognising which bell belonged to which church. Sometimes they sounded more distinct than others — it depended on the weather and the wind and the time of day. It would become more difficult to sort them out later on in the morning when the cascading peals of St Patrick's and Christchurch joined in.

The smell of fry wafting in from the kitchen made Kate's nose twitch. She hopped out of the bed and dressed quickly. Seated at the kitchen table, her father was already half-way through his breakfast, with Saturday's *Evening Mail* propped up against a milk bottle. Wearing her best hat and coat, Mrs Doyle was on the point of leaving for eight o'clock Mass. 'There's a bit of fried bread and a rasher keeping hot there on a plate, if you want them,' she said to Kate. 'Make yourself a fresh drop of tea and have the potatoes and cabbage washed before I get back, like a good girl.

Danny, don't forget to bring in a few more logs and a bucket of turf as soon as you're finished.'

'Right, ma.' Kate lifted the big black kettle off the hob and placed it carefully on the fire. Immediately, it began to sing.

As soon as Mrs Doyle had departed, Mr Doyle looked up from his paper. 'I'm afraid you'll be losing Dusty this week, Kate. There's not a trace of the thrush this morning, so tomorrow you can take her around to Ned's to be shod.'

Kate stopped chewing her fried bread. 'Is she going back tomorrow then? I thought she was staying until Buck was better. And what about her stable — hasn't that still to be fixed up?'

'Well, Buck has made a remarkable recovery, thanks to your mother. He's still a bit stiff but last night he started taking a few steps and he's hoping to venture out into the yard today. As for the stable, I'm going to tackle that later on today. It shouldn't take long if Jamie and his pals give me a hand. But I won't let Dusty go back before Wednesday.'

'How are you going to make sure that Buck takes care of her properly? You know yourself that he won't groom her.'

'I had a long chat with him last night and he promised to make the effort, and to give him his due, he hasn't had a drink since the accident. Anyway, you'll still have to groom her — even when she's back with Buck — until he's fully recovered himself that is.'

Kate knew that her father was doing what he thought best in the circumstances. Although having to go to Buck's every day didn't appeal to her, she accepted that, in Dusty's interest, it had to be done.

When Mrs Doyle returned from Mass she was agog with excitement. 'Wait till you see what's in the Sunday paper — a huge, big photo of Kate driving Amber past the GPO. Look, right there on the front page. Isn't it only gorgeous?'

Kate looked over her father's shoulder at the photograph. She could hardly believe her eyes. Printed underneath, for all the world to see, were the words, 'The most beautiful participant in the Pony Express Protest Parade, filly-foal Amber, owned by Mr Danny Doyle, and driven by his thirteen-year-old daughter, Kate.'

'Well, that bates Banagher,' exclaimed Mr Doyle in disbelief. 'How in the name of fortune did they find out who we were?'

Mrs Doyle couldn't take her eyes off the picture. 'Will you look at Nora waving at the crowd. It's really beautiful.'

'We'll have to cut it out and put it up on the wall,' said Kate.

'Better still,' said her father, 'I'll go into the newspaper office tomorrow and buy the photograph. I don't care how much it costs — I'll just have to have it. The only pity is that you're not in it, Madge. Wait till Ned and the others see this.'

The picture set the tone for the day. It lifted everyone's spirits. Kate couldn't remember when she had been so happy. All the upsets of the past two weeks were completely forgotten. To cap it all, later that evening, her father brought back good news from Ned's about the campaign.

A public meeting was to be held in the Mansion

House in the very near future, at which a number of well-known personalities would speak. In the meantime, an all-out effort was to be made to get as much support as possible from the public. To this end, the various animal humane societies were drawing up a programme of action called the 'Five Ps': Parades, Posters, Protest Meetings, Publicity and Politics.

'It looks as though there's a busy summer ahead of us,' Mr Doyle predicted goodhumouredly, 'so I'll be relying on you, Kate, to give a hand out whenever possible. Now that yourself and Amber have hit the headlines we'll have to devise some means of making use of it.'

'Now, don't go losing the run of yourself,' Mrs Doyle warned. 'You seem to be overlooking the fact that I'll need help here in the house, besides which, Kate will have to look ahead to the future. She has only a few months left now before she'll be out looking for work. See how well young Lila Keogh didn't let the grass grow under her feet; she's far too cute.'

It hurt Kate to the quick whenever her mother spoke like that. She felt that such a comparison between herself and Lila was insulting to both of them. It was very unfair, she thought, especially when her mother knew quite well that Lila had no say whatsoever in the matter. Custom forbade her to answer back — she would only be accused of being cheeky, so instead she decided to go to bed and let her father argue the point.

It was gloomy in the bedroom although there was still a certain amount of light in the evening sky.

Jamie was sitting up in bed reading the *Our Boys* with the aid of a tiny altar-lamp. Whacker and Nora were fast asleep.

'You know that you're not supposed to have that lamp in the bed,' Kate said, trying to work off her irritation. 'The place could go on fire.'

Jamie looked up. 'What's the matter with you? You've a face on you that would turn milk sour.'

Kate went over to the window and pulled aside a corner of the lace curtain to get a better view of the yard outside. She heaved a long-drawn-out sigh.

'It's ma. I'm sick and tired of her nagging me about going to the sewing when I leave school. She knows perfectly well that I'd prefer working with da and Amber. And I wouldn't mind but it's all because she doesn't think it's a job for a girl. I can't understand how it was all right for me to help da up to now and then it suddenly becomes all wrong.' She sat down on the edge of the bed and looked over at Jamie. 'I wish to God I was you. You don't know how lucky you are being a boy.'

'Lucky! You must be joking,' Jamie burst out indignantly. 'I don't want to work with da when I leave school. All that mullockin' around with horse-shit and mucky vegetables would drive me bonkers.'

'Ah, you're just bone lazy. All you want to do is rear pigeons. What use is that going to be to you?'

'Is that so, smart aleck? A lot you know about what I want or don't want. Well, for your information, rearing pigeons is only a hobby. And as for what I'd like to be, well, I'd like to be a carpenter. Only I can't. See? Trades happen to run in families and da isn't a carpenter. So there.' With that he blew out the altar-lamp and sank beneath the bedclothes.

Kate lay awake for a long time turning over in her mind what Jamie had said. Never before had she heard him express the slightest interest in work of any description. It came as a complete surprise to her to discover that, like herself, he nursed a secret ambition to be something that was really very ordinary, but yet, for some reason, was unattainable. The more she tried to make sense of it, the more incomprehensible it became.

Nine

On Monday morning, Kate walked Dusty slowly and carefully to Coyne's forge to be shod. Ned couldn't believe the difference in the mare's appearance. He ran his hand over her silky coat, noting how much she had fleshed out under Kate's tender care.

'You've the makings of a vet in you, Kate, and no mistake. But sure, it wasn't off the ground you licked it. That father of yours is better than any horse-doctor I know and signs on it that you take after him. Not indeed,' he quickly added, 'that you're ever likely, no more than himself, to become one.'

Kate had to smile at Ned's bluntness but his remarks reminded her of the conversation with Jamie the previous night. They made her wonder if her father had harboured any ambitions to be a vet when he was young. It was something else for her to find out.

Monday was usually a quiet day in the forge. Ned's son had the day off so Ned was working alone. When he began filing and shaping Dusty's hooves, the little mare's legs began to quiver nervously. Kate held her by the halter and whispered reassuringly into her ear.

All her life, Kate had been coming to the forge with her father. Like all young people in the area, she found it fascinating to watch Ned as he quietly went about his work. The whole scene was so highly dramatic and at times very tense, especially if he was dealing with a difficult or sensitive animal. On more than one occasion Ned had been sent flying across the forge by a mighty kick but Ned was brave and he never allowed a mean horse to get the better of him.

Holding Dusty's foot firmly between his knees, he deftly pared away the surplus growth of horn with the rasp and coarse file. Kate wondered how such big, strong arms and hands could be so gentle one minute and display such strength and force the next. Sparks flew in all directions as the hammer hit the red-hot shoe on the anvil. The water hissed like an angry snake when the shoe was plunged in the vat. Then the acrid smell of burning horn filled the forge as Ned applied the shoe to Dusty's hoof for size.

The heat in the forge became unbearable. Ned's shirt was soaked in sweat and rivulets of water ran down his cheeks. Kate had to stand at the entrance to cool herself. 'It wouldn't surprise me if we had thunder,' Ned remarked, drawing the back of his huge, hairy hand across his forehead. He looked at Kate's red face framed by her long, red hair, and laughed. 'Here,' he said, lifting up his rubber apron and rummaging in his trouser pocket, 'run across the road and get yourself an ice-cream before you melt.'

On the way back from the shop, Kate met Lila's mother pushing a dilapidated high pram laden with clothes. She was on her way to the Iveagh Market wash-house to do the weekly load. Round her shoulders was an old, threadbare, black shawl. Her silvery hair was pulled tightly back from her face and wound into a bun at the back of her head. Her most notable feature was her skin, which was the colour of putty because of a chronic liver problem.

Although only in her mid-fifties, she looked much older. She nodded at Kate and gave her a toothless smile.

'Hello, Mrs Keogh. Is Lila back yet?'

Mrs Keogh slowed down but didn't stop. 'No, thank God,' she said, crossing herself and lifting her eyes to heaven. 'Let's hope that's a good sign. If the power of prayer works she's got the job because I haven't stopped. Why don't you call around after tea this evening and she'll tell you all about it.' Then, as if to console Kate for her unemployed status, she added cheerfully, 'Sure you won't feel the time passing before you'll be out earning yourself, please God.'

By the time Kate got back to the forge, Ned had just finished putting on Dusty's last shoe. 'Take her nice and easy going back,' he advised. 'Avoid the cobblestones. Go the long way home — it'll give her a bit of exercise. Her oul' muscles are a bit on the slack side.'

Going up Braithwaite Street, Kate saw two men walking slowly in her direction. As they came closer, something about them seemed familiar. They stood and stared at Dusty as she passed by. Only then did Kate recognise them. They were the two men she had seen giving the money to Buck in Johnny Power's pub.

Her heart began to race with fear. At the corner of Summer Street she looked back. They were on their way up after her. As soon as she rounded the corner and entered the yard she closed over the gates and rushed Dusty into the stable. Peeping out through a crack in the gate, she saw the men standing in the middle of the road looking thoroughly puzzled at her sudden disappearance.

Her mother's head appeared over the half-door. 'What in the name of fortune are you shutting the gate for? Don't you know your father will be back any minute with the dray and he's not going to be pleased if he can't come straight through?'

Kate put her finger up to her lips. 'Shh. It's your men — the Pony Express scouts,' she whispered, coming nearer the door. 'They're after following me up the street.'

Inside, Kate explained what had happened. Mrs Doyle's face clouded over. 'Maybe they're looking for your father. I only hope to God that he's delayed. Do you think they recognised you?'

'They couldn't have. They never saw me that night. It's Dusty they recognised, and even at that they weren't sure, because she looks so different. What are we going to do? They'll kill da if they see him alone.'

Mrs Doyle stood motionless for a minute, her hand up to her face. Then she turned to Whacker. 'Open the wicket-gate gently and have a look up the street. Careful now.'

Whacker did as he was told, delighted to be playing the detective. There was no one in sight.

'Right,' said his mother, 'look round the corner and see if they've gone back down Braithwaite Street. If they have, race on ahead of them and warn your father. He'll be coming from Ardee Street direction. With any luck they've gone down Marrowbone Lane.'

There was no sign of the men but Whacker remained at the corner until he saw his father in the distance. He raced back to inform Kate, who then opened the yard gate.

When Mr Doyle heard Kate's story he praised her quick thinking. 'Them go-boys are up to something, mark you me. I wouldn't be a bit surprised to hear that they've already been to see Buck. As soon as I've the bit of dinner taken, I'll pop around to check.'

The click of the wicket-gate latch sent Kate rushing out into the yard, but it was only Jamie.

'What's the big idea of shutting the blinking gate?' he roared indignantly. 'I can't get my box-car through.'

'Keep your hair on, for heaven's sake,' Kate replied sharply, pulling aside the bolt. Jamie dragged the box-car into the yard. It was full to the brim with stout bottles and jam-jars which clinked and rattled as they bumped and bounced over the cobblestones. Very carefully he lowered the shafts down outside the door.

'I cleared them all out, ma,' he called inside to his mother. 'Buck says I can keep half of what I get for them. Look, there's only millions worth there.' He rubbed his hands together with relish.

'Good man, Jamie,' said his mother. 'You did a great job. It'll make a big difference to have them gone. Now, come here till I ask you a question. Did any men come to see Buck while you were there?'

'Yes, two. I was sawing the wood for Dusty's stable at the time. One went into the cottage to Buck and the other stayed outside watching me. I didn't like the look of him and when he asked me what I was doing

91

I said 'sawing wood'. Jamie burst out laughing. 'You should've seen his face — he nearly blew a gasket. I thought he was going to give me a belt but lucky for me, Buck happened to come out into the yard.'

'Have you any idea what they wanted?' his father asked.

'No, but when they had gone, Buck said for you to call around as soon as possible, that it was important.'

'Did they ask where Dusty was?'

'Yes, but Buck only said she was being shod.'

Mr Doyle scraped his chair back from the table. 'Kate, you'll have to do the rest of the deliveries today. There aren't many and they're all in Rialto. Jamie, you'll have to come with me.'

'But, da, I want to go to Harry Sive's to get the money back on the bottles and jam-jars. Buck told me not to delay.'

Mr Doyle drew a deep breath and heaved a long sigh. 'For God's sake, don't try my patience, Jamie. There are far more important things to be done right now. Follow me around to Buck's when you've eaten your dinner — and bring a few of your pals. I can do with all the help I can get with the stable before the weather breaks.'

'Who are the mèn anyway?'

'They're the gougers who tried to buy Dusty for the Pony Express. Keep an eye out for them around the area. They're bad news.'

Buck confirmed Mr Doyle's suspicions. The two were trying to persuade him again to sell Dusty but he had refused. When they adopted a threatening attitude, he became alarmed. 'They said if I didn't sell, they'd make it hot and heavy for me. They've given me a few days to make up my mind.'

'We'll just have to be very vigilant,' said Mr Doyle. 'It's a pity we don't know where they're based because then we could put the gardaí on them. One thing for sure, though, I'm going to put a good bolt and padlock on the stable door in case they try any funny tricks.'

After tea that evening, Kate went to see Lila. Standing well out on the road, she cupped her mouth in her hands and hollered her name up to the open window. Mrs Keogh poked her head out, leaning her elbows on the sill.

'You'll have to come up, Kate,' she shouted down. 'She's half-dead after her day's work and isn't able to put a foot under her.'

Kate traipsed all the way up to the top floor of the tenement where Lila's mother rented two rooms. She had to keep close to the wall because part of the bannisters was missing and the rickety wooden stairs creaked and groaned at every step. Just as she mounted the last flight of stairs, a door opened and Mrs Keogh appeared on the landing, holding a chipped and rusted enamel basin.

'She's over in the room beyant, Kate, prostrate on the bed. Since she came home she hasn't stopped complaining. One minute it's her feet and the next it's her head, then it's her finger. She has my heart scalded listening to her. I wonder would you mind bringing that drop of lukewarm water over to her because I swear to God, if I hear any more out of her, I'll drown her with it.'

Kate smiled and took the basin. Mrs Keogh raised

the latch and Kate entered a room in which there were three beds and nothing else. They were all the room could hold. A small uncurtained window with four squares of glass was set deep in the wall overlooking the back yard. One of the squares was broken, another cracked. Over each bed hung a holy picture, one of the Sacred Heart, one of the Holy Family and another of St Thérèse. Lila lay rolled in a ball on the bed beneath St Thérèse. She looked up at Kate and groaned. Kate placed the basin down on the floor.

'I don't think I'll ever be able to put my feet to the ground again. Look at my ankles — the size of them. All day long I'm standing. The oul geezer of a forewoman wouldn't let me sit down.'

Kate burst out laughing and sat on the end of the bed. 'You certainly look all done in. What's all this about not being able to sit down? How can you work a sewing-machine standing up?'

'Sewing-machine! I wasn't near any sewing-machine, for God's sake. Clipping threads off shirts and carrying bales of material into the cutting-room, that's what I was doing all day. My arms and my back are aching like mad and as for my head — I thought it was going to explode from the clickety-clack of the power belt and the screeches and bangs of the machines.'

Kate had never seen Lila looking so exhausted. 'Maybe it's just something you have to get used to. You mightn't feel so bad after a while — that's if you stick it out.

'Stick it! I'll have to — I've no choice. Me ma would do her nut if I left. And it's not just the standing. The forewoman is a real oul' battle-axe. Everyone is terrified of her. All day long she's shouting and bawling and half the time I don't know what she's saying. She's from Derry and she has this funny accent. But you should see her. She looks ancient and wears this long, black dress and a wide, black belt laden with millions of keys and an enormous scissors. I think she's an escaped warden from Mountjoy.'

Lila's spirits revived as she went on to describe the horrors of her first day and before long the two friends were rolling on the bed laughing.

'No one's allowed talk or sing. I thought school was bad but this place takes the biscuit altogether; it's like a reformatory. And just take a gawk at my finger from the scissors. Did you ever, in all your life, see such a welt?'

When Kate got home she recounted to her mother all that had happened to Lila in the factory. She took care not to embellish it with humour, as Lila had done, hoping that the cruel, naked truth would help dampen her mother's ardour for the sewing. In this she was disappointed.

'Sure it stands to reason that she'd be jaded — it's only her first day after all. And you've got to take into account that Lila is inclined to be a bit on the delicate side. You won't have them problems — you're used to hard work, and besides, by the time you start, you'll already know the machine — you won't be a red-raw rookie like Lila.'

With a heavy heart, Kate went outside to check on the ponies. Her mind was all of a muddle. Nothing seemed simple any more. There was Lila, and all she wanted to do was sing. Jamie wanted only to be a carpenter. She herself just wanted to work with horses. Yet, for reasons she could not understand, there were impediments in the way. She knew that lack of money was one, especially in Lila's case, but it wasn't the only one. Who decided, for instance, that because her father wasn't a carpenter, Jamie couldn't be one? And why did her mother believe that working at the sewing was a more acceptable occupation for a girl than working with horses?

She stood at the half-door of Dusty's stable listening to the sleeping pony's steady breathing. It saddened her to think that the little mare would soon be back with Buck. Even though looking after her had taken a lot of time and hard work, it had been both enjoyable and rewarding. Lila's description of the factory sprang into her to mind: the noise, the stuffy atmosphere, the boredom, the strict discipline, the fear of the forewoman. She didn't know how she would ever come to terms with such a regime. It just didn't bear thinking about. If only she could be like Lila and laugh it all away.

Ten

The following evening Kate's father arrived home with two copies of the parade photograph and the morning paper, which contained another investigative article on the Pony Express. One of the photographs was for Ned Coyne's forge. Kate's mother measured them and promised to buy frames in Woolworths at the earliest possible opportunity.

Mr Doyle waited until Kate was busy with the ponies and Mrs Doyle had gone to check on Buck, then taking the paper from his inside coat-pocket he sat down by the window.

A photograph with the article showed the corpse of a little Irish pony, lying in the yard of the slaughterhouse at Vaugirard, a suburb south-west of Paris. It had been skinned, and for some reason it now lay partially crushed under the wheels of a meat truck. The reporter described how he witnessed a draught-horse being led to slaughter, past dead and bleeding animals. The horse trembled when it saw others being skinned and then panicked when it heard the hollow thwack of a heavy cleaver splitting open a skull. The terrified animal was quickly subdued by the stinging lash of a whip with metal thongs.

The remainder of the article dealt with the economics of the trade, especially the huge profits being made by those involved in horse-smuggling across the Irish border.

Mr Doyle found the article so upsetting himself that he was in two minds whether or not to show it to Kate. It was so much more explicit than the first report had been. Every gory detail was described. He lit his pipe and sucked gently on the stem, sending tiny puffs of smoke into the air. Through the window he could see Kate as she bedded the ponies down for the night. It was wonderful, he thought, how well she could handle them and the way they responded to her. For a while he sat there giving free rein to his thoughts.

Remembering his own youth, he could easily identify with Kate's hopes and ambitions. What she wanted is what he had wanted — to work with sick and injured animals. To do that required money and education. Still, he hadn't done too badly. Over the years he had learned, through experience and tips from vets, how to treat minor injuries and more importantly, how to care properly for horses. He could see that it wasn't going to be so easy for Kate. In fact, it was going to be well-nigh impossible. That was just how things were. Nevertheless, he hadn't it in his heart to discourage her by supporting her mother's traditional views on what was right and proper.

The Pony Express Campaign could be the answer to the problem. It would give her an outlet, a chance to become involved in animal welfare, he considered. That would require more than just an emotional reaction to the cruelty and horror of the horsemeat trade. She would have to be well versed in all the facts in order to counteract the propaganda and expose the clique who controlled and operated it. The only way she could do that was to read the article.

Kate came in from the yard. He folded the paper before handing it to her.

'Another article this morning,' he said. 'Don't read it now – take it into bed; I don't want your mother attacking me for upsetting you. You will find it very gruesome, but it's important that you know the facts.'

Kate went inside to the bedroom and put the paper under her pillow. When she came back out, Jamie and her mother had just come in the door.

'You can see the evenings are drawing in already,' Mrs Doyle remarked as she searched for a spare nail behind the door on which to hang her coat. 'Only a few weeks ago it was broad daylight at this time and now look at it – it's nearly dark. Light the lamp there, Danny, till I see what I'm doing.'

Mr Doyle lifted the glass globe off the Aladdin oil-lamp and placed it gently on the table, then he turned up the wick. As soon as the match-flame touched the mantle it popped into light. Before replacing the globe he took care to lower the flame. The soft light suffused the room.

Jamie was all smiles. 'What's up with you?' asked Kate. 'You're like the cat that got the cream.'

'And sure, why wouldn't he?' replied his mother. 'Isn't Buck after giving him a fortune. Go on, show them.'

Jamie extended his open palm. It held three half-crowns. Kate looked incredulous. 'Seven and sixpence! Why did Buck give you all that?'

'It's the half of what I got for the Guinness bottles and jam-jars.'

'There must've been only millions.'

'Sure it was like a brewery around there. I don't know how many times I filled the box-car.'

'What are you going to do with all that money?' his father asked.

'Spend it, of course.'

His mother looked indignant. 'You'll do nothing of the sort, me bucko. That's a small fortune. Tomorrow morning you'll go straight up to Thomas Street Post Office and get yourself a savings book. Your Confirmation is coming up next year and that money can go towards it.'

Jamie's jaw dropped. 'Aw, ma. Can I not keep some of it?'

'A shilling — that's as much as you're keeping and even that's too much for a child of your age. What would you do only squander it on sweets and comics.'

With that Jamie had to be content. His father said nothing. Money was Mrs Doyle's department.

In the bedroom, Jamie complained bitterly but Kate didn't listen. She sat up in the bed reading the article. Her stomach nearly turned over. She kept thinking of Dusty and the narrow escape she had. Those two men today were up to something. She wished her da wouldn't send Dusty back to Buck. Again and again she asked herself how human beings could be so cruel to animals. The campaign was all very well but while it was going on, thousands more horses were being tortured and slaughtered. She felt frustrated and helpless.

Sleep was impossible. Nora felt like a furnace. Kate moved nearer the edge of the bed but it was no cooler. After a few minutes she gently pulled off the blanket, leaving only the sheet. She remembered that Lila hadn't called as promised. Maybe she was too exhausted. Poor Lila, cooped up in that awful factory especially in this hot weather. And that forewoman shouting and bawling at her all day. Lila said all she was short of was a whip.

The snorting of the ponies woke her up next morning. Nora was already sitting at the kitchen table eating a bowl of stirabout.

'You're up early,' Kate remarked.

Nora looked sulky. 'Well, I couldn't sleep with you. You kept on kicking me and talking in your sleep.'

Kate laughed and tousled her sister's hair. 'I must've been having a bad dream.'

'It's all this heat,' said Mrs Doyle as she fanned the fire into life with the bellows. 'And if there isn't a bit of wind soon to blow away the smell of the knacker's we'll all be smothered. How anyone can think that smell is healthy beats me.'

'Where's da?'

'Miles Cassidy called around at six o'clock and asked him to have a look at one of his cows. It has an abscess on its teat. He should be back any minute but you'd better get on with feeding the ponies.'

Kate went out into the yard and rinsed the water-buckets. As soon as they heard the splashing sound, the two ponies poked their heads over the half-doors and whinnied. While the buckets were filling, Kate spoke to them and stroked their faces. After steadying the buckets in the centre of two old car tyres she led

101

the ponies in turn out into the yard. They rubbed necks and nuzzled affectionately. While they quenched their thirst, she mucked out the stables.

By the time her father returned from Cassidy's dairy-yard, Amber was fed, groomed and ready for the road. Kate lingered over Dusty's grooming, paying attention to every little detail. Then she took the mare for a short walk around the block.

Even at this early hour there were plenty of people abroad: Guinness men changing shifts, dockers on their way to the canal harbour, hauliers, carters and cyclists, all vying for space on the narrow roads. Most of them she knew very well, the rest just to see. In Thomas Court Bawn she came across Paddy Doyle from Maryland, with his box-cart and four buckets, shovelling up the early morning horse-dung for his prize roses. He always tried to get it done early on Wednesdays before the sheep and cattle, on their way to the slaughterhouses from Cattle Market, had time to leave the roads in a slippery, slimy mess.

Later in the morning, she took Dusty home to Buck's. Turning into the Green Yard the mare came to a sudden halt, refusing to budge an inch. She whinnied and tossed her head, prancing nervously on her front legs. Kate pressed her head into the pony's neck. She could feel the heart pounding. It wasn't until after much stroking and coaxing that the mare allowed herself to be led forward up the lane.

Buck was nowhere in evidence. The yard was cleaner than Kate had ever seen it and the floor of the new stable was strewn with plenty of fresh straw. The structure itself was roomy enough to allow Dusty to turn around in comfort. It even had a small window high up on the wall near the door. A tethering ring and a thick, tarred hay-net were the only wall-fittings. Mr Doyle had run out of timber for the roof but Buck told him where he could pick up sheets of corrugated iron cheaply. These had still to be covered with roofing felt, which Buck hoped to obtain for nothing as soon as he and Dusty were back in business.

Dusty inspected every corner of her new quarters. With dilated nostrils she puffed hard into the air, tossing her head as if in disbelief. Kate was equally impressed. Satisfied that the little mare was at last going to be comfortably housed, she tethered her to the ring and went over to the cottage to see Buck.

The door was open and she found him sitting at the table drinking a mug of tea. His face was still discoloured and his right hand was heavily bandaged. The room looked clean and neat. Without the piles of papers, dirty clothes, bottles and jam-jars, it was surprisingly spacious.

She stood on the threshold. 'Dusty's back. I've left her in the stable.'

Buck nodded, muttered something, but made no move to rise.

'She's groomed and fed. I'll be back in the afternoon to take her round the block again. Da said he will call after dinner and ma will be here later on this morning.'

Buck raised his hand in acknowledgement. Kate hesitated for a few moments before turning to go. His indifference to Dusty's return upset her. Before leaving the yard she bolted the half-door of the stable. Dusty shifted nervously on her feet, her big, soft brown eyes full of apprehension. Kate gave her a final hug and ran all the way home, fighting back the tears.

Between helping her mother with the sewing, her father with Amber, and Buck with Dusty, Kate hadn't a minute to spare over the next few days. She was happy enough, except during the sewing sessions. Then her thoughts would turn to Lila, who hadn't called to see her after work, as promised.

On Friday the weather finally broke. At first the showers were intermittent, with huge raindrops as big as half-crowns splattering the city streets. As the day advanced a steady downpour developed. By evening it was coming down in torrents. Dark, clouds hung low in the sky. The flooded streets were deserted.

Kate was sitting in the kitchen reading a comic to Nora. Jamie was sprawled on the floor with Whacker playing a game of Snap. Mr Doyle was checking his market list for next day and Mrs Doyle was ironing clothes. Suddenly the room was illuminated by a flash of lightning. Almost immediately a low rumble of thunder rolled across the sky and burst in a deafening climax overhead. Nora screamed and Whacker dived under the table.

'Merciful heavens!' cried Mrs Doyle, crossing herself. 'The Lord between us and all harm.' Nora rushed over to her mother for protection. Jamie stood up and went over to the window.

'Come back away from there,' his mother shouted in alarm. 'You could be struck down dead.'

Mr Doyle cocked his head sideways. 'Whisht, is that Amber I hear?'

Above the noise of rain and thunder could be heard

a high-pitched whinnying. Mr Doyle jumped up. 'I'd better go out and check. She's probably frightened out of her wits.'

Kate immediately thought of Dusty. What if she too were frightened? Buck wouldn't care one iota. She could kick up as much fuss as she liked but he wouldn't put himself out in any way on her behalf. It was some consolation to know that on a night such as this, she would at least be dry and comfortable.

And safe. The bolts and locks her father had put on had been made specially by Ned Coyne so there was no danger of Dusty disappearing like Mickey Mulligan's cob.

Gradually the storm abated and everyone became more relaxed. Thunder could still be heard but it was away somewhere in the distance and the rain had almost ceased. Mrs Doyle finally persuaded the children that it was now safe to go to bed; that the end of the world had not yet come. Whacker was full of questions as to where the thunder and lightning came from. His mother said it was God's way of showing that he was angry with the world. Whacker said that God must have a fierce temper. Jamie said that he knew for a fact that the thunder was the noise of Guinness's barrels rolling across the sky and that when they crashed all these sparks of lightning shot into the air. Mr Doyle said he didn't know for sure where it all came from, it had something to do with electricity and that only scientists understood it properly, but one thing he did know was that it must've done a powerful amount of damage.

'Wait till tomorrow and then we'll know all about it. I wouldn't be a bit surprised if lives were lost. One thing I'm glad of anyway, and that's that I got Dusty's stable finished in time. I'll have to go around there first thing in the morning to check out if it has stood up to the storm.'

Eleven

When the first clap of thunder rumbled overhead, Buck was in bed. He had exerted himself so much, lifting and scattering bales of straw all over the stable floor in preparation for Dusty's arrival, that he had to retire earlier than usual. As well as that, his injured hand had begun to ache badly from lifting some heavy planks in out of the rain.

Shortly after Kate's departure, he had decided to have a look at Dusty. It was easy to tell by the way her ears stood stiffly forward that she was feeling apprehensive about something. Her big, wide eyes showed mostly white as they scanned the cloud-laden sky. When she saw him approaching, she backed nervously into the stable. The minute he opened the half-door, she tossed her head and uttered short frightened snorts and began pawing the ground.

Her improved appearance surprised him. A look more of avarice than of admiration gleamed in his eyes as he tried to assess the price she might fetch at the coming monthly horse fair over in Smithfield.

Bending down to have a look at her new shoes, he grabbed her leg roughly and attempted to lift it. She resisted and kicked her leg forward instead. The jerk

107

sent such a painful dart up Buck's right arm that he lost his temper. 'Hoho, getting uppity now, are we? Well, I'll soon put manners on you, me fine lady, don't you worry.'

At the sound of Buck's voice, Dusty's ears bent back almost flat against her head and her tail swished furiously. Buck looked around for the whip, which he eventually found outside in the cart.

For a few moments the two eyed each other, then with a shrug, Buck turned away, and threw the whip into the corner. He lacked the energy to assert his authority, and besides, his wrist was too sore. There'd be other times to teach her who was master.

He bolted the two halves of the door but couldn't remember where he had put the key to the padlock. Danny had been most insistent that he be sure to lock up at night in view of the threat from the Pony Express scouts. While he was searching about in the gloomy kitchen, there was another heavy downpour of rain. 'Ah, to hell with it,' he muttered impatiently. 'Only them that'd be out of their senses would be abroad on an night like this.' Without even bothering to remove his clothes, he fell down wearily on the bed and fell fast asleep.

For a moment after being woken by the thunderbolt, Buck thought there had been an explosion. When the room was illuminated by a flash of lightning and more loud rumbles of thunder, he realised he hadn't been blown to pieces. The ferocity of the storm didn't worry him in the slightest but he was fuming with rage at having his sleep disturbed.

To make matters worse, the torrential rain bombarding the corrugated roof of Dusty's stable sounded more like a deluge of marbles and he could hear her neighing and whinnying with fright. In an effort to reduce the noise level, he covered his head with the pillow but it was so hot he had to take it off. There was nothing for it but to smoke a Wild Woodbine until the storm passed. He reckoned that once the elements returned to normal, so too, would Dusty.

This was not to be, however. If anything the mare got worse, until finally, Buck couldn't stick it any longer. He rose in a fury, intending to whip her into silence. Holding a small flashlamp he stepped out into the rain-flooded yard. To his utter amazement the stable door was wide open and Dusty seemed to be going berserk inside. Then he heard a man's voice pleading with someone to 'hurry and get up off the bloody floor and stop acting the maggot.' A low moan was the only answer.

Buck immediately switched off the flashlamp and quietly approached the stable door. While his eyes were becoming accustomed to the darkness, he heard the man's voice again.

'For Christ's sake, Ledner, will you get a move on! I can't see a bloody thing and I'm up to my knees in water trying to hold the bloody door open.' This time there was no reply at all.

Suddenly Buck's voice rang out. 'What the blazes are you up to, you young cur. Horse-stealing, is it?'

He made to grab the man but the man swung round and struck him with his closed fist on the jaw. Buck went down like an empty sack and while he lay stunned on the ground the man kicked him several times.

Believing he had got the better of Buck, he turned his attention again to his friend. Buck tried to get to his feet and his hand came in contact with the whip. Drawing it backwards, he made to strike the man on the back of the head with the handle but a sudden weakness caused him to fall down. Wrenching the whip from Buck's hand, the man lashed out viciously.

The leather thong cut into Buck's face and he collapsed, screaming with pain. Just as he was about to strike again, Dusty, who all this time had been neighing and jumping about in terror, reared up on her hind legs and with a ferocious kick, sent the man flying out into the yard, where he landed heavily, face downwards, in a pool of water. He groaned a few times and then lay quite still.

With considerable pain and effort, Buck managed to raise himself into a sitting position. Blood was pouring from his nose and one of his eyes wouldn't open. His whole face was smarting from the weal made by the whip. Thinking he was going to be sick he lay down again, clasping his face in his hands, and curled himself up into a ball on the blood-soaked straw. His head was pounding so hard that it was some time before he became aware of the warm, wet nose nudging him gently in the back of the neck. At first, he thought it was his imagination, but no, there it was again and this time the nudge was accompanied by soft whinnying.

All Buck could do was lie there and let it happen. Gradually, his body began to relax as the soothing caresses of Dusty's nose took effect. Her obvious concern for him filled him with shame and remorse. He thought of how cruel and callous he had been to her all her life, and of how he had come out only minutes before to whip her, instead of wanting to calm her. He cringed in mental agony as some of his past acts of brutality flashed before his mind. In the course of these cogitations, he felt as if his whole being was undergoing the exorcism of some terrible fiend. He reached up his good hand and, for the first time ever, he stroked the little mare fondly on the nose.

After a while, his mind began to clear. He remembered that the man had addressed someone named Ledner. Where was he? It was too dark to see — he'd have to find the torch. With great difficulty, he crawled along the ground, scrabbling about in the straw, until he eventually found it.

After a few sweeps, the weak, flickering light picked up the form of the man lying out in the yard. There was no movement from him. Buck got to his feet and steadied himself against the wall for a moment because his leg hurt. He shone the light over Dusty and gently patted her shoulder. She was making funny breathing noises and her coat was beaded in sweat. Then the light caught a pool of blood on the ground by her hind legs. He discovered the mare had a large gash in her right hind leg, extending from the cannon bone to the hock. It was bleeding badly. Then he noticed the body lying at the back of the stable and when he shone the light on the face he recognised one of the men who had wanted to buy Dusty.

His initial concern was for the mare. She was obviously in a state of shock so he made his way through the flood, over to the cottage, and returned with a blanket. After he had her covered he brought her a bucket of water. Then he limped as fast as his aches and pains would allow to get help from Danny Doyle.

The sight of the lamplight shining through the Doyles' kitchen window filled him with relief. At least he wouldn't be rousing them from their sleep and help would be all the quicker.

Inside, Kate and her parents were having a much-needed cup of tea after having finally calmed the younger children and got them to sleep. When Buck's loud banging came on the door, the three of them exchanged questioning glances. Kate rose and opened the top half of the door. The sight she beheld caused her to reel back in terror. Her first thought was that Dracula himself had come back from the grave. Screaming with fright, she dashed over to her parents at the fire.

Without uttering a word, Buck reached over, unbolted the bottom half of the door and entered the kitchen. Kate's parents were so shocked by Buck's bloody and dishevelled appearance that for a moment neither of them could speak. Mrs Doyle was the first to recover and immediately took things in hand.

'In the name of God, Buck, what's after happening to you?' She led him over to the fire and seated him down on an easy-chair.

'Here, drink this mug of tea before you collapse. You'd better get them wet clothes off before you catch your death. Kate, run inside and get a few of your father's duds out of the wardrobe; whatever comes to hand.'

Buck took a gulp from the mug, then put his hand

112

up to halt Mrs Doyle's fussing. 'There's no time for any of that, Maisie, thanks all the same. Danny, you'll have to come around quick. Dusty is badly injured. I think she's bleeding to death.' He clutched Mr Doyle's arm and his voice shook. 'She saved my life, Danny, she saved my life. You've got to do something to save hers.'

Kate could hardly believe her ears. Could this possibly be the Buck she had known and feared all her life? With the blood dripping profusely from his facial wounds, his whole appearance looked ten times worse than she had ever seen it. Yet, it spite of his red swollen eye and the large weal stretching from ear to ear, his rain-sodden clothes and the dirt, he no longer instilled fear in her. As his story of the attempted kidnapping and struggle unfolded, she realised that Dusty had succeeded, by her swift defensive action and sympathy, where her father had failed, with his appeals and threats.

Mr Doyle wasted no time. He could see that Buck was in no fit condition to make the short journey back to the Green Yard on foot so he told Kate to yoke Amber up to the trap. Mrs Doyle did her utmost to persuade Buck to remain and have his face washed with disinfectant but he refused. Kate wanted to accompany her father and Buck but her mother asked her was she out of her mind and told her to go straight to bed.

In the space of a few minutes, Amber had them back in Buck's yard and with the aid if his powerful torch Mr Doyle surveyed the scene in and around the stable. He could hardly believe his eyes.

The man Dusty had kicked out into the yard was

now moaning in pain, soaked to the skin. Mr Doyle tried to move him out of the pool of water into the stable but he yelled out in agony. Asked if he could move by himself, he uttered a faint 'no'. Danny put some straw under his head and over his body and then went to look at Ledner.

He was lying on his back with his eyes closed. He felt warmer than his companion, due to the fact that he was dry and had the advantage of warmth from Dusty, but Mr Doyle could see that he was unconscious, although there was no obvious sign of injury.

Next, he turned his attention to Dusty. She was lying down and he could tell at a glance that she was in great distress. The wound in her leg looked serious, with the blood pumping out in regular pulses. It was clearly a job for the vet but until his arrival it was essential to reduce the flow of blood. This Mr Doyle did with a thick wad of clean gauze. Leaving Buck in charge, he jumped into the trap, galloped Amber around into Braithwaite Street and woke up Mr Brennan, the publican. Here, he made three phone calls, one to Newmarket Garda Station, one for an ambulance and the third for Mr Lawless, the vet.

The ambulance and the Black Maria arrived simultaneously and in no time at all, the ambulance men had Ledner and his companion onto stretchers. After examining Buck's face they insisted that he accompany them also. He was reluctant but Mr Doyle pointed out that there were two very good reasons for going to the hospital. 'One is that you need to have your eye and face attended to and the other is that you've got to be able to prove that you were attacked.'

'We'll follow on to the Adelaide and take the necessary statements,' said the garda in charge, 'but first we'll take a look around here and have a word with Mr Doyle.'

Mr Doyle told them all he knew, which was very little. While he was showing them the injury to Dusty's leg the vet arrived. 'What we would like to ascertain,' the garda said in an important voice, 'is whether the wound was deliberately inflicted or was the result of an accident. The answer to that will be crucial to our investigations, because if it is the former, those two boys could get a fair stretch in Mountjoy.'

Mr Lawless was able to state right away that the injury had been deliberately inflicted. 'In fact,' he said, holding up a worm-eaten plank he had found nearby, 'this is the weapon. Look at the size of that nail — and it's covered with blood.'

Satisfied for the moment with their investigations, the gardai departed for the hospital, taking with them the whip and the plank as important pieces of evidence.

The vet asked if Dusty had ever been immunised against tetanus.

'I doubt it,' said Mr Doyle. 'Buck wouldn't be a man for taking precautions against anything.'

After stitching and bandaging the wound, the vet left, promising to be back in a few hours. 'It's getting on for three o'clock now and we all need some sleep after such a dreadful night. The mare is to be kept quiet and there's to be no movement whatsoever or the healing will be delayed.'

When everyone had left Mr Doyle considered the situation. God only knows how long Buck was going to be in the hospital. Then the gardai would be waiting to take a statement from him. Dusty just couldn't be left alone. There was nothing for it — he would have to stay the night.

He was too tired to give any thought to comfort. As long as he could lie down, that was all he wanted. It was necessary for him to have a light all night in the stable so he brought Buck's paraffin-oil lamp from the house and hung it on a nail near the door. Then he unyoked Amber and led her in. The moment she entered the stable the smell of blood hit her nostrils and she made to draw back, but catching sight of her mother prostrate on the floor, she changed her mind. Dusty, exhausted by her traumatic experience and drowsy from the injections, was hardly aware of her filly's presence. Amber fussed around for a while before lowering herself down onto the straw with her face close to her mother's. Finally, satisfied that everything had been attended to, Mr Doyle carefully lowered the wick of the lamp until the light was reduced to a tiny, yellow glow.

Twelve

When Mrs Doyle realised next morning that Mr Doyle hadn't come home all night she became alarmed. Hastening into the children's bedroom she roused Kate from her sleep and told her to dress quickly and dash around to Buck's to find out what was the matter.

By this time the rain had stopped but the narrow streets were badly flooded because the drains had been unable to cope with the extra volume of water. In some places it was so bad that Kate had to wade carefully to prevent it from pouring over the tops of her boots. Mopping-up operations were already under way in low-lying shops and homes as people frantically tried to salvage food, furniture and personal belongings from the rising water.

Kate found Buck's yard in a terrible mess with loose debris of every description scattered all over the place. The sight of Amber's trap was reassuring but when there was no reply to her loud knock on the door, she became slightly uneasy.

'Da, are you in there?' she called. 'It's me, Kate.' When there was still no reply, she lifted the latch and pushed open the door. Inside, she found the cottage empty. The only sound was that of water drip, drip, dripping from a leak in the roof down into a bucket standing over near Buck's bed. The regular plopping sound and the emptiness gave the cottage an eerie atmosphere and made Kate shiver.

Coming back out into the yard, she noticed the top half of the stable door slightly ajar so she made her way over, choosing a route that obliged her to jump across two wide puddles, just to prove that she could.

Even before she thrust her head into the stable, she could hear the familiar sound of Amber's snoring. The pony's sensitive ears flicked and her eyes opened as soon as she became aware of Kate's presence. Dusty remained asleep. While Kate was sliding back the bolts, Amber gave herself several vigorous head-shakes before rising to greet her. With her head close to the filly's face, Kate was whispering her usual words of affection, when her eyes fell on a human form lying on its side in the straw. Her heart missed a beat. For a moment she didn't recognise who it was but as soon as she did she feared the worst — that he had been injured or killed. She threw herself down on her knees beside him.

'Da, da, are you all right, da? It's me, Kate.' She shook him hard and pulled him over onto his back. To her relief his arms flew upwards and he muttered a few incoherent words of protest at being so roughly disturbed from his slumbers.

'Ma sent me around to see if you were all right. What happened? Why didn't you come home? Where's Buck?'

Mr Doyle pulled himself up into a sitting position and blinked several times. He gazed slowly all around the stable. 'Where on earth am I at all, at all?'

He covered his face with his hands and groaned, 'Oh, my head. It feels like it's about to burst.'

'You're in Buck's, in Dusty's stable. Do you not remember what happened last night? Remember the thunderstorm, and Buck all covered in blood, and Dusty and the kidnappers?'

The full horror of the night came rushing back into Mr Doyle's brain. Slowly he ran his fingers through his hair, then he rolled sideways and pushed himself up onto his feet. A factory hooter sounded in the distance.

'What time is it, do you know?'

'It must be about seven o'clock. You'd better get back home because ma nearly had a fit when she found you hadn't returned.'

Mr Doyle nodded over towards the mare. 'I still can't leave Dusty. The poor thing has about thirty stitches in her leg and she's lost a lot of blood.'

Kate knelt down and stroked Dusty's neck. 'Poor little Dusty. Will she be all right, da? It's terrible that she's just got over one thing and now this has to happen.' A hopeful note came into her voice and her face lit up. 'We'll have to take her back home with us again, won't we?'

'I'm afraid not, Kate; she can't be moved until the stitches have knitted the wound together. If it's a thing that Buck is kept in hospital, I'll stay here with her myself until she's on her feet. Anyway, it's a bit previous to be making any predictions till we have word from the hospital.'

Outside, Amber was showing signs of hunger, so Mr Doyle picked up a bucket and began filling it at the tap. Kate could see how tired and weary he looked. While the filly was drinking he went inside the cottage to light the fire.

'I'll do all that, da. Why don't you go on home and have your breakfast; ma will be mad if you don't. She was getting it ready when I was leaving. You can bring Amber back as well and get Jamie to feed her. I'll take care of Dusty — just tell me what to do.'

For a moment her father hesitated. Then he gave her a pat on the shoulder. 'You're right. A cup of tea and a bit of grub wouldn't go amiss. It's just that I don't like to leave you all alone with such a sick pony.' He took a long look at Dusty before finally making up his mind. 'I don't think there's any danger of her even trying to get on her feet — she's too weak and a bit drowsy from the injections. If she does wake, get her to drink some water out of a shallow basin. I'll be as quick as I can.'

It took Kate ages to get the fire going because the turf and sticks were so wet, but when she eventually succeeded in creating a cheery blaze, she felt that it had been well worth the effort. Between tidying the room and running outside to keep a check on Dusty, she didn't feel the time passing.

Shortly before her father returned, accompanied by Jamie, the mare woke up. Kate could see by her eyes that she was in pain. She made no attempt to move, so Kate brought over the basin of water and helped to hold her head up while she drank. Mr Doyle handed Kate a bag containing an egg sandwich and a flask of tea. 'Your mother said you had no breakfast, so get yourself outside of that.' He then took Dusty's temperature and covered her over with a clean blanket which he had brought with him. 'It's normal, thank God. With a bit of luck she'll pull through without any complications. What I'm worried about more than anything is that the wound might go septic. If it does she's in real trouble.'

With the minimum of disturbance to Dusty, they cleared the stable of all the blood-stained straw. Jamie was in his element, being so close to the scene of the crime. 'Wait till the gang hears that Buck knocked the stuffing out of the two robbers. They just won't believe it. Ay da, is it all right if I bring them up later on to see Dusty's sore leg?'

'You'll do nothing of the sort,' his father retorted. 'And furthermore, you're not to be letting your imagination run away with you. Even Buck doesn't know how the Ledner fella was knocked unconscious and it was Dusty and not Buck who let fly at the other guy. So I'm warning you, Jamie, no spreading rumours, OK?'

Jamie looked very crestfallen at this injunction. He had been looking forward so much to boasting to all his friends about the family involvement in the midnight adventure in which he had every intention of casting himself in a leading role. As if he could read Jamie's mind, his father smiled and winked at Kate.

'Believe me, Jamie, the real story is just as exciting as anything you could make up. Later on, you can come down with me to Newmarket Garda Station and we'll find out the score on the robbers and then we'll visit Buck in the Adelaide Hospital. The vet should be here shortly to check on Dusty and we'll go after that.'

The prospect of visiting the garda station and the

hospital revived Jamie's spirits. Things were getting more and more exciting. He thought the vet would never arrive.

Mr Lawless was pleased with Dusty's condition. 'She's remained stable, which is a very good sign,' he said when he had taken her temperature. 'That means that the wound hasn't gone septic and that she's responding very well to the treatment. I'll give her another injection to help kill the pain and keep her from moving about. Any news from the hospital yet about Buck and the two men?'

While her father and the vet discussed the night's stormy events, Kate busied herself preparing a light feed for Dusty. She heard Mr Lawless say, in answer to a question from her father, that the pony had obviously kicked Ledner unconscious after he had injured her leg.

'I wouldn't say she did it on purpose,' he added. 'She simply reacted to the pain and shock by kicking out with her hind legs after he attacked her. He just didn't get out of the way quickly enough.'

'Buck will be relieved to hear that, I can tell you. With his history, he could easily be accused of having done it.'

'Even if he had,' said the vet, 'he would've been perfectly within his rights. After all, wasn't he only trying to save his pony from kidnapping? Which reminds me, how is the campaign going?'

'We've a public meeting next week in the Mansion House, to put pressure on the government to have the Pony Express debated in the Dail. Some opposition TDs and other public representatives have agreed to speak. You'd be more than welcome yourself, Mr

Lawless. Someone with a professional knowledge of horses and the effects this cruel form of exportation has on them would be a great asset to us.' Mr Doyle took a leaflet from his pocket. 'Here you are, take this to remind yourself of the date.'

'I'll do my best, Danny, but no promises, because I never know what will turn up. If you let me have more leaflets I'll leave them lying about in the surgery.'

'Thanks, Mr Lawless. I'll run Kate over this afternoon with a bundle.'

The vet smiled at Kate. Unknown to her, he had been watching the way she handled Dusty and spoke to her. 'I can see you have a way with animals, Kate. Dusty doesn't know how lucky she is.' Kate blushed with embarrassment at the unexpected compliment.

'She absolutely fantastic with horses,' Mr Doyle announced proudly. 'Spends all her spare time grooming and caring for our own pony, who by the way, happens to be Dusty's filly. And for the last couple of weeks she's been caring for Dusty also. You see, Buck is inclined to be very careless with the mare and she picked up a foot infection. He has a bit of a drink problem, if you know what I mean.'

Mr Lawless looked at Kate with interest. 'So you like horses, Kate. I could do with someone like you to help out in the surgery. Nowadays it's so very hard to get anyone really good to take on the work.' With a click he closed his leather bag and consulted his pocket-watch. 'I must be off now, Danny. I'll call again tomorrow morning. Don't forget those leaflets, Kate. Bye now.'

Kate could hardly think straight with excitement.

After seeing the vet to the gate, her father returned all smiles. 'Well now — what do you make of that? It's an ill-wind that doesn't blow somebody some good. I think you made quite an impression there, Kate.'

'Do you think he was serious, da, or just being nice?'

'Oh, he was serious all right — he isn't usually that friendly. He even asked me outside how old you are and he seemed a bit disappointed when I told him you still had six more months to go in school. I'd say that if you'd been old enough he'd have offered you a job there and then. There's no doubt but these fellows always have their eyes to business.'

'Do you have any idea what kind of work he'd give me, da?'

'Oh, general dogsbody, I suppose. All these professionals need unqualified people to do the menial tasks to enable them to get on with the more important things. But like everything else, if you like being involved with animals, these things have to be done. Now, take my advice, say nothing to your mother about it. There's no point in worrying her and besides, nothing might ever come of it.'

Jamie came rushing in to announce that he had cleared the drains, swept the yard and collected all the rubbish. 'Right,' said his father, 'we'll head off for the hospital, so. You run on, Jamie, and start yolking Amber up to the trap. We won't be long, Kate.'

They were gone only a short time when the neighbours began calling into Buck's yard to find out about the attempted kidnapping. In spite of all precautions the news had spread like wildfire through the neighbourhood. Each caller had a different version of the night's drama — there was even one who said he'd heard that Buck had actually murdered one of the kidnappers and was now being held in Newmarket Garda Station!

Eventually, Jamie returned alone. He told Kate that Buck was being allowed home and that his father was waiting in the hospital for him. 'You should see him, Kate. He'd frighten the daylights out of you. I thought he was bad before, when he looked like Dracula, but now he's the spittin' image of the mummy in *The Mystery of the Wax Museum*. Remember the way the mummy's face was all rolled up in these bandages — well, all you can see of Buck is his mouth and one eye.'

Although Kate had to laugh at Jamie's description, she was quite shocked at Buck's appearance. Part of one side of his face was visible and very badly discoloured. The bandage circled his head at a slant, holding a bulky dressing in place over his damaged eye. With her father's help he dismounted from the trap and limped slowly and unsteadily into the cottage but he was only in the door when he turned around to go out again.

'Just a minute, Buck,' said Mr Doyle, catching him by the arm. 'Where do you think you're off to?'

'I must go and see Dusty,' Buck replied, shaking himself free. 'I want to be sure she's going to be all right.'

'You know very well she's going to be all right, Buck. I told you so a million times already. Now come on in and have a cup of tea and a rest. Dusty is out for the count after her injection. She'll be in better form when she wakes up, so leave it until then.'

Reluctantly Buck allowed himself to be led in again. With a deep sigh, he flopped down into a chair by the fire and accepted, mechanically, the cup of tea handed to him by Kate.

'How many stitches did you say she got, Danny?'

'Thirty. It seems a lot, but it's not really; I've seen horses with more and there wasn't a bother on them later.'

Buck put his hand up to his bandaged face. After a moment he spoke. His voice was unusually low. 'You know, Danny, I've been thinking things over about last night and I'm absolutely convinced that your man would've whipped me to death only for Dusty. She saved my life although she was very badly injured herself.' His voice faltered. 'And then, to crown all, she tried to tell me how sorry she was that I was hurt. I'll never forget that moment as along as I live.'

For the first time in her life, Kate believed that Buck meant what he was saying. She was sure he now realised that Dusty had attacked the man with the whip because she knew only too well what it felt like to be lashed mercilessly herself. It suddenly occurred to Kate that she really ought to say something on Dusty's behalf and at the same time let Buck know that she understood what he was feeling.

'Animals are like that, Buck. They don't bear grudges like humans do. Dusty is also a very intelligent pony and she probably sensed that the kidnappers were up to no good.' Then she added with a laugh, 'Maybe she heard us talking about the Pony Express and was only making sure that she wasn't going to be put on it.'

Whatever Buck may have thought of her remarks, he didn't say anything. Mr Doyle rose and went outside to see if Dusty was awake but she wasn't. He suggested to Buck that he take a lie-down and was relieved when he agreed.

Kate was eager for news of the kidnappers. 'Well,' said her father, 'I'm very happy to say that Ledner regained consciousness, and it has been definitely confirmed that the blow to his head was caused by a kick from a horse's hoof. As well as that, the two gurriers have been charged with the attempted kidnapping of Dusty and will be appearing in court shortly. All this, of course, is going to be great publicity for the campaign. Which reminds me, you'd better go back and get a bite to eat before running over to the vet with the leaflets.'

Thirteen

Over the weekend, the Green Yard was a hive of activity, with sightseers from all over the neighbourhood wanting to get a glimpse of Buck and Dusty. Some of them came to wish Buck well but most simply wanted to satisfy their curiosity. Adding to the confusion were the reporters and photographers from all the national papers.

Kate happened to be in the stable with Dusty when some of them arrived. Several photographs of herself and the mare were taken, all of which appeared in the newspapers the next day. Buck, however refused to meed anyone, leaving all statements on the Pony Express and the background to the attempted kidnapping to Mr Doyle.

The photograph of the injured mare aroused much public sympathy. Her role in saving Buck's life and in bringing down the thieves was highly praised. It was all great publicity for the campaign and Kate's father made use of it to the full.

Things seemed to be moving at such a rate that Kate could hardly keep up with them. One thing in particular made her feel very happy and that was her visit to the vet's surgery. Mr Lawless had shown her around and he had even allowed her to stay to watch a cat being neutered! 'I'm glad to see that you're not a bit squeamish,' he remarked when she was leaving. 'I was half-afraid that you might faint. Thank your father for the leaflets. Just leave them with the receptionist and tell her to give one to everyone who comes in.'

On her way home, she called to see Lila to tell her all the news. 'Where have you been all week?' Kate demanded. 'Every time I call around you're either at work or gone out. I'm beginning to think that you must be avoiding me or something.'

'Will you look at who's talking!' Lila replied in mock-indignation. 'You're spending so much time with your four-footed friends that you're beginning to look like one, especially round the gob.' She burst out laughing and Kate gave her a frinedly jab with her elbow.

'It's all this blinkin' overtime,' Lila continued. 'It's taken over my life and it's going to last until the end of July.'

'What! You don't mean to tell me that we're not going to be able to see each other for even one night? What's all this overtime for, anyway?'

'It's because the factory is closing down for two weeks' holidays at the beginning of August and the boss wants all the orders out by then. And, to make bad worse, I'm not entitled to any holiday pay because I'm not there long enough. Me ma, of course, is glad of the overtime money, because it'll help to tide her over the two weeks.'

'And what about the machine? Any news about when you'll be put on one?'

'Well, if the examiner is anything to go by, I'll be

standing clipping threads for the next six months at least. That's if I don't die of boredom or suffocation in the meantime. There's all this lime or starch comes flying out of the material when it's going through the machines and it makes the air as thick as pea-soup. The roof is a great big dome of glass and when the sun shines it's like being in a hothouse — it's awful.'

After hearing this and more about Lila's bad working conditions, Kate hadn't the heart to tell her that the vet had offered her a job in his surgery. To do so might make it appear as if she were boasting. Not that there was any certainty about it — her mother might very well put her foot down and that would be the end of it. Time enough to tell her when she knew definitely one way or the other.

The evening before the Mansion House meeting, Kit Lane came rushing into the Doyles' yard waving a newspaper excitedly in the air. 'There was holy open desolation down at the quayside in Fishguard this morning,' he announced breathlessly. 'One hundred and ninety-two donkeys arrived there, *en route* for Italy, to board the Pony Express. By the time they reached Fishguard, thirteen of the poor animals were dead! Fortunately, a picket from the International League for the Protection of Horses was there and wouldn't allow the remaining donkeys to go on board. Instead, after a lot of hassle, they bought the rest for £1,600!'

Mr Doyle read out the report. It stated that this was one of the worst cases of suffering in the traffic of donkeys to date. An English veterinary surgeon had examined the animals and found that some had no teeth and could not graze, all had eczema and many had lice. A post-mortem examination on the dead donkeys showed that most were over twenty years of age and had diseased internal organs.

There was a long silence when Mr Doyle finished reading. Kate had covered her face with her hands. Her mother sat quietly at the sewing-machine. Kit Lane was the first to speak.

'I'm beginning to lose heart, Danny. Things seem to be getting worse. As far as I can see, we're never going to stop the Pony Express unless we're prepared to take some kind of drastic action. Otherwise the government is going to continue turning the blind eye to all this cruelty.'

'Don't despair, Kit. I know things are looking very grim right now but it's all grist to the mill. After tomorrow night's meeting, I bet you two to one that the government will begin to take a great deal of notice of us.'

While the men continued to discuss the government's refusal to debate the issue, Kate couldn't get the fate of the donkeys out of her mind. She thought the people who had bought them were the nicest people in the world. All she wanted to do now was to go to Fishguard, wherever it was, and help them look after the one hundred and nine donkeys that remained.

'What's going to happen to all those donkeys now, da?' she enquired anxiously.

'Oh, I expect that those that are able will be put to work and the rest will live somewhere in quiet retirement. But it's not the answer to the problem, Kate. The animal humane societies couldn't afford to go on indefinitely buying all the animals sent for slaughter. That would create more problems than it would solve. The only solution is for the government to ban the Pony Express. That's what we want and we'll not stop till it's achieved.'

Kit Lane looked doleful. 'I only hope to God that tomorrow's meeting will be well attended. If not, I'm afraid you can throw your oul' hat at it.'

But Kit need not have worried. The meeting was a huge success with over one thousand people packing the Round Room of the Mansion House. When Mr Doyle returned home he was jubilant. Kate and her mother were waiting up to hear all the news.

'I never saw so many people in all my life. Half of them couldn't get into the hall. They came from everywhere — some of them big noises, too. Several of the speakers had travelled on the boats with the animals and were able to give eye-witness accounts of the conditions on board and it would break your heart to hear them. Of course, there were those who weren't in the least bit interested in the cruelty — business people who see export on the hoof as a terrible loss to the country. In the end they are the ones who'll make the government change its policy.'

Then Mr Doyle's face lit up. 'I've kept the best news until the end. The attack on Dusty and Buck was mentioned by someone as an example of the unscrupulous methods employed by Mr Big's scouts, and I was called upon to give an account of what happened. I needn't tell you, I nearly died with fright when I got up on the platform, but once I got started, I forgot the fear. You should've heard all the clapping when I'd finished. Then, didn't one of the speakers suggest that Dusty be rewarded for her bravery and for the part she played in saving Buck and capturing the kidnappers!'

At this piece of news, Kate's eyes opened wide with delight. 'You mean to say that Dusty is going to get money, da? How much? And when?'

'Well, the committee is to decide on a day and venue for the presentation of the reward but I doubt very much that it'll be money. I expect she'll get a rosette or a medal or a cup or something like that. Anyway, it'll be a great excuse for a big celebration and God only knows we need something to cheer us all up.'

The following morning, Kate was over in Buck's grooming Dusty when the vet arrived. 'She's looking splendid, Kate,' he said, running his hand over the mare's silky coat. 'You'd easily know by the way she's progressing that she comes from a good, spirited, fighting stock.'

Kate beamed. 'She's getting a reward, Mr Lawless, and there's going to be a big ceremony, so I want her to look her best.'

'Yes, I was at the meeting myself last night and Dusty's name was on everybody's lips. She's quite famous now and it's no more than she deserves. Now then, I think it's time I had a look at the leg to see how the wound is knitting together, so if you'll hold her steady, I'll remove the bandage.'

Mr Lawless carefully examined the wound. 'There you are — a nice neat job, don't you think?'

Kate bent down to see. The mark of the stitches looked like a long piece of barbed wire embedded into Dusty's leg. Kate thought the wound looked awful but she didn't like to say so. 'It's lovely, Mr

Lawless, but will it always look like that?'

The vet gave a hearty laugh. 'Don't worry, Kate. After a while you'll hardly notice the marks, Now, if you get me my snippers out of my bag, I'll remove the stitches right now.'

Dusty never moved a muscle while Mr Lawless gently and deftly snipped away at the wire. Satisfied that all was well, he told Kate to put a halter on and take the pony around the yard. 'Only a little walk for the moment until she gets her strength back. While you're doing that, I'll go over to tell Buck that I've removed the stitches, but before I leave I'd like to have a word with you.'

Dusty seemed glad to be rid of the bandage and was quite reluctant to go back into the stable after one round of the yard. She stood snorting outside the cottage door until finally Buck and the vet emerged to see what all the fuss was about. At the sight of Buck, she moved forward and nuzzled him in the shoulder. Buck stroked her face gently. Kate handed him the halter rope. 'Here, Buck, I think she wants you to take her back.' Dusty obediently turned at Buck's command and the two of them limped slowly over towards the stable.

Kate smiled at the vet. 'You wanted to see me about something, Mr Lawless?'

'Oh, yes. I was wondering if you had given any thought to what I said the other day about working for me. I've already spoken to your father and he tells me you'll be leaving school after Christmas. I can see you have a way with animals — it's a gift really — and it would be a pity if you let it go to waste. What do you say?'

For a few moments Kate couldn't say anything. Finally she found her voice. 'Oh, I'd love to, Mr Lawless, but you see, my mother wouldn't let me 'cause she doesn't think it's the right kind of work for me. She wants me to go to the sewing and have a trade, just like she has.'

Mr Lawless rubbed his chin thoughfully. 'I could have a word with your mother. She probably thinks the work would be messy and dirty, but it's not. My receptionist is leaving in a few months to get married and I'm going to need someone to take her place. Although a lot of it is paperwork, the job needs someone able to deal with the animals as they come in. I know you'd be perfect for the job. Just leave it to me. I'll find some way of bringing her around.'

Kate was estatic. Everything was turning out so well. For the first time since the school holidays had begun, she experienced a warm, comfortable feeling of wellbeing. Dusty's health and safety were now assured and, although Buck's injuries were slow to heal, his personality had undergone a dramatic improvement. The campaign was gaining support, and soon, with any luck, the Pony Express would end. And in a week or so, Lila would be on holidays from the factory and life would become carefree again.

That afternoon, Mr Doyle called into Ned Coyne's forge. Ned greeted him with delight. 'Ah, the very man I want to see. The news is only after coming through that the Dáil has at last fixed a date to debate the Pony Express.'

When he was told the date, Mr Doyle burst out laughing. 'Well, if we'd arranged it we couldn't have done better. It's on the same date as the court hearing! I was coming around to tell you that Buck and myself have been subpoenaed to appear and I wanted you to round up as many people as possible for support on the day. I'm going to notify the newspapers myself so that we'll get the maximum amount of publicity.'

The following day on her way back from Buck's, Kate called into the newsagents for her *Girls Crystal*. Deeply immersed in the latest escapades of the Terrible Twins of the Sixth Form at St Melva's, she didn't notice the figure approaching until they collided. Looking up, she discovered Lila blocking her way.

'Lila! What are you doing? Why aren't you at work?'

'I've been sacked.'

'Sacked! When? What for?'

'Just before lunchtime. I couldn't stick the oul' reprobate of a forewoman any longer. She ordered me to carry a big bale of material into the cutting-room and I refused. I told her it was too heavy and that it wasn't my job. You should've heard her. Anyway, she accused me of all kinds of bad behaviour and said that I was nothing but the scum of the earth. That was enough. I just picked up an empty cob and let fly at her. It caught her right in the gob. Before I knew it, she'd thrown me out into the lane and told me never to darken the door again.'

Kate looked at Lila in disbelief. Suddenly Lila burst out laughing and linked her arm through Kate's. 'Don't look so shocked. I felt great after throwing the cob. If it had been a hatchet, I would've thrown it just as quick. She had it coming to her.'

'That's not what I'm thinking of. It's your ma. What's she going to say when you tell her you've no job?'

'She already knows. She took it very well. I think she realised that I wasn't going to be put on a machine and the wages were very small. Anyway she's often said that I'd be better off in England with my big sister. She has a good job on the railway and ma is going to write and ask her to try and get me in.'

'You mean you'd be going to England?' Kate thought she was hearing things. 'And when would that be?'

'Well, not for a few weeks, anyway. Me ma hasn't written yet, and me sister will have to make enquiries and so on.' She looked at Kate's glum face and gave her arm a squeeze. 'Cheer up, for God's sake. I thought you'd be glad to hear that I was out of the factory. We'll be able to have a bit of gas for the next few weeks.'

All Kate wanted to do was cry. The thoughts of Lila emigrating was such a shock that she felt like getting sick. How Lila could talk about it so casually was beyond her comprehension. She did her best to hide her feelings and together they walked around to Summer Street, arm-in-arm, as they had always done before. It was as if nothing in the world had changed.

That night, Kate lay in bed looking up at the cracks in the ceiling criss-crossing one another. They were going nowhere, yet everywhere. They had no beginning or end. She remembered how, long ago, she was able to make patterns and shapes out of them, but now they were just a jumble.

The bombshell that Lila had dropped about

emigrating had shattered her completely. Just when she had thought that things were beginning to return to normal, this had to happen. She wondered how it was that Lila was able to take everything in her stride while she just fell to pieces.

The events of the last few weeks passed before her mind. She had to admit that in spite of her present gloomy feelings, there had been some important changes and improvements. The future wasn't looking nearly as bleak as it had been. Mr Lawless had spoken to her mother during the day and she had agreed, reluctantly, to allow Kate to take the job after Christmas. Two black spots clouded the horizon. One was the Pony Express which was still in operation – although not for long, she hoped. The other was Lila's imminent departure for England. She wished with all her heart that she could do for Lila what she had done for Dusty – keep her at home.

> *Other wonderful books*
> *from*
> *Attic Press young adult*
> **BRIGHT SPARKS** *series.*

HAS ANYONE SEEN HEATHER?
Mary Rose Callaghan

Fast-moving THRILLER about two Irish teenage sisters' search for their mother, **Heather Kelly**, last heard of somewhere in London.

An absolutely believable story which tugs at the heart strings as **Clare** and **Katie** discover that life in London is no bed of roses.

'A thoroughly up-to-date teenage book . . . a breakthrough in Irish literature.' Margrit Cruickshank *The Irish Times*

Winner of Reading Association of Ireland Special Merit Award

£4.99

DAISY CHAIN WAR
Joan O'Neill

Set during the late thirties and early forties, this is the heartwarming story of cousins, Irish **Lizzie** and English **Vicky**, growing up during 'The Emergency'.

'An eye-opener for the young reader and a nostalgic treat for the older one.' Robert Dunbar *The Irish Times*

'An exciting story about growing up during 'The Emergency' in Dublin. Definitely a good read for girls of twelve and over.' Blathnaid Archer *Sunday Press*.

£4.99

I'M A VEGETARIAN
Bernadette Leach

A true to life funny and sad story of the fights, fears and friends of rebellious **Vanessa Carter** who discovers that coming to live in Ireland means learning a whole new way of life.

'This, I have to say, is a treasure of a book.' Vincent Lawrence *Sunday Press*.

£3.99

SUMMER WITHOUT MUM
Bernadette Leach

Explore the further adventures of **Vanessa Carter,** the fourteen-year-old girl from *I'm a Vegetarian*, who decides to make her own plans when her mum gets an offer to go and teach in America for the summer ...

Vanessa dreams of freedom, fun and adventure in a *Summer Without Mum*, a summer which turns out to be full of adventure and excitement for this rebellious teenager, but not quite the sort of excitement she had planned.

£4.99

WELCOMING THE FRENCH
Geraldine Mitchell

When thirteen-year-old Gemma decides to help a group of young French refugees to enjoy a holiday in Connemara in the West of Ireland, she never imagines that her life could become so complicated or that things could go so wrong.

As busloads of French teenagers arrive in Gemma's town she thinks that all eventualities have been catered for. Everything goes well until two of them go missing ... !

£3.99

Attic Press hopes you enjoyed **Pony Express**.
To help us improve the **BRIGHT SPARKS** series for you please answer the following questions.

1. Did you enjoy this book? Why?

_____

_____

_____

2. Where did you buy it?

_____

_____

_____

3. What did you think about the cover?

_____

_____

_____

4. Have you ever read any other books in the BRIGHT SPARKS series? Which one/s?

_____

_____

_____

If there is not enough space for your answers on this coupon continue on a sheet of paper and attach it to the coupon.
Post this coupon to **Attic Press**, 4 Upper Mount Street, Dublin 2 and we'll send you a **BRIGHT SPARKS** bookmark.

Name_____

Address_____

_____